Infinite Weekend

Denise DeMarco

Dedication: For everyone else who ever cheered for the knights at the Renaissance Faire, and made memories to last a lifetime. This one's for you.

Chapter 1

Lance

Lance typically avoided making idle conversation. When you worked at the Renaissance Festival–even for part of the short season–the job required you to interact with people and to stay in character. Given the number of giddy attendees, tipsy travelers, and day trippers letting down their hair, that might occasionally be fun–if his real reason for being there wasn't so damn far from funny.

As he walked, he kept his stride long and purposeful. It discouraged conversation and fit his character. A medieval knight getting ready to joust didn't have time for small talk. Neither did a man on a mission, especially a covert one.

Lance veered to the right around the huge mud "stage" where a group of actors/acrobats performed several times a day. Watching the dressed and half-dressed performers do their thing in squelching mud was amusing the first couple of times. After that, even seeing a couple of them gargle with the stuff wasn't enough to keep his attention.

While spectators were waiting for the next mud-encrusted performance, they were focusing on a trio of wandering minstrels at one end of the performance area and jugglers at the other. Without his Dark Knight attire, most visitors didn't recognize him as part of the wildly popular joust. Instead, as an "ordinary" knight, he could've been an enthusiastic spectator who dressed for the occasion, like many other visitors.

When he circled around the mud stage and left the crowd behind, Lance stayed to the right. He ducked behind the small, striped tent housing a vendor selling frozen whips of orange juice and lemonade. No IED danger here, just electrical wires leading back to a generator that had to be hidden behind the tree line. Festival management was committed to preserving an authentic look whenever possible.

Lance kept moving further into the trees, taking another sharp left and deeper into the property owned by the festival. The sounds around him changed, became quieter now. He was away from the big shows and closer to the last designated rest area. All that was out here were a few picnic tables, a bottled water vending machine, and a couple of portable toilets that the management called "comfort stations." They were hidden inside distinctive, blue-striped tents. Today's meeting spot was 30 meters beyond the last one.

After positioning himself with his back to a sturdy tree so he had something at his six, Lance continued to listen for his contact. He mentally counted off minutes and tuned out the distant sounds of the festival. Finally, rustling and a bird call came to him from his right. He returned it, and moments later, a man came into view.

"Nice day," the newcomer said.

"Yeah."

They shook hands. Though Lance was loath to touch the guy, it added to their cover and obscured the transfer. He palmed the thumb drive passed to him. After another minute of innocuous conversation, Lance was alone again. He bent to adjust his boot tops and dropped the drive into the right one. As much as he wanted to check the contents, he couldn't leave the fairgrounds for several hours yet.

The Dark Knight was scheduled for another joust today.

Chapter 2

Callie

As her playlist began the next to last song, "The Champion," Callie flicked the blinker on and turned into the gravel driveway. Her GPS had been accurate, and the drive had taken about three hours to get from Long Island to Sterling Woods.

She hadn't gotten on the road until later than she'd wanted, so now, the late summer sun was already setting. The big Victorian-style mansion that housed the B&B was a perfect storybook image, complete with gingerbread latticework and a couple of towers rising from the upper floors. In the waning sunlight, the building looked like something out of a dream. Or on a postcard.

A carved signpost in the driveway indicated that visitors checking in should pull into the parking spots allocated in front of the building. There was space for two vehicles, and both spots were empty; another indication that it was a small establishment, despite the size of the house. The website told her there were cottages on the property, as well, but not how many.

Well, if she had to take a forced vacation, at least this place was picturesque, if nothing else. Hopefully the guest rooms were similarly welcoming. She was going to relax, maybe do some sightseeing, and recharge her internal batteries. Then she'd return to work. For the next year, she'd be able to cite this trip as proof she *did* take time off.

Callie turned off the car, grabbed her purse off the passenger seat, and slipped her phone in the outer pocket. Solar lights nestled in the bushes were coming alive, sending their glow reaching gently upward. There were only three front stairs, but they were wide, stretching a third of the way across the expanse of the front porch.

The front door of the inn was as pretty as the rest of the façade; the wooden door and brass hardware warm and inviting. When she pushed the door open, the tinkling sound of a welcoming bell announced her arrival. The softly lit interior was scented with roses and vanilla, and there was a soothing backdrop of gentle music.

"Welcome! I'll be with you shortly."

For some reason, Callie had expected there to be an elderly woman at the reception desk. A woman stood, marking things on a paper map for a man in his 60s, but she wasn't at all the grandmotherly type. Her glossy hair was cut in a stylish bob. Her makeup was on point, even in the muted light, and her fingernails were long. She looked like she'd be more at ease working in a Manhattan hotel than in a local bed and breakfast in upstate New York.

The man folded the paper and was on his way, walking toward the rear of the lobby space.

The woman behind the desk focused her attention on Callie. "I'm Melody, and welcome to Orchard Corners. How can I help you today?"

"I'm checking in. Callie Stewart." Callie slid the necessary items across the desk to her.

"Glad you made it," Melody said, already typing on her computer. "I'll need photo ID and a credit card for our records."

Melody made quick work of processing the paperwork. After Melody handed everything back, she said, "We had a guest leave unexpectedly, so you have a choice of rooms. I can give you either a room here in the house or one of the outside cabins."

That was unexpected. Everything she'd checked in the area had been fully booked or nearly so. Callie tried to remember the descriptions of the accommodations outside the house.

"Sorry, I'm trying to remember the descriptions of the cabins."

Melody leaned closer across the space between them and lowered her voice. "The cabins have a variety of themes, but they're all like little escapes from the every day. The one I can give you is seriously relaxing."

Relaxing was the goal for her week in the area. "How much more expensive is it?"

When Melody named a number far less than what Callie expected, she looked at her incredulously. "That's it?"

"With the 'from one working woman to another' discount, yes."

Callie hesitated only a moment longer before she laughingly accepted. "Thank you. I'm not good at relaxing, so I can use all the help I can get."

"Guests staying in the outer rooms have access to the same room service, housekeeping, and other services as guests staying in the rooms in the house do." Melody slid a small folio over. "This contains two guest keys. They give you access to your cabin, and to the main house. We serve a continental breakfast in here every morning, or you can order room service to have something brought to you."

Before Callie could ask how to find her cabin, Melody was already explaining. "Are you parked in the registration spots near the front door here?"

"Yes."

"Okay. From there, you'll continue past the house and follow the gravel road. There are a good number of cabins, so check the number on your folio and follow the signs. Even when it's completely dark, you'll be able to see what you need to. We have a well-lit drive and reflective numbers."

Barely fifteen minutes later, Callie was on the little front porch of cabin eight. Like Melody promised, it'd been easy to find. The outside of the cabin, visible because of the exterior lighting, was a unique blend of rustic styling and Victorian touches like the gingerbread trim found on the main house.

Callie unlocked the door with more excitement than trepidation.

The interior welcomed her with warmth and surprisingly luxurious details. A cellophane wrapped gift basket rested in the middle of the coffee table in front of the plush couch. Callie peaked into it enough to see gourmet teas and coffees, snacks and candy. A soft as cashmere throw was folded along the back of the couch. The decorative pillows were crafted of butter-soft fabrics. Resting her head upon them was hard to resist.

Callie wandered through the two-bedroom cabin, admiring the luxe fabrics and decadent surprises like chocolates in the bathroom, on a tray next to a bottle of sparkling wine in a silver pocket, all positioned by the clawfoot tub.

Despite her initial reluctance, this definitely had the potential to be a memorable experience.

The next day, after a good rest, Callie headed up to the main house to make a plan of sorts. She needed to find food. The B&B served breakfast and evening snacks, although she'd fallen asleep too early yesterday to walk back to the main house and sample them. When she woke up this morning, cocooned in the billowy comforter, Callie admitted to herself that her boss might've been right, and she needed a break from work.

Callie helped herself to a cup of coffee from the round lacquered table set up near the reception desk in the lobby of the main house. The plate of what looked to be freshly baked cookies was tempting, but she bypassed it; she might be on vacation, but breakfast should still come first. She'd grab some area brochures and promotions to look at over the breakfast she intended to enjoy in the dining room.

Coffee firmly in hand, Callie walked across the lobby to the alcove where she'd spotted the visitor material. There, she was disappointed to discover that the brochures on the shelves of the wood rack didn't look promising. A doll museum looked creepy. A toy train collection didn't interest her at all. Same for the collection of 19th and 20th century quilting and embroidery; she'd enjoy it for 15 minutes and then be ready to move on. The next few brochures were more appealing. She considered pumpkin farms, apple orchards, a corn maze, some place that hosted Victorian-style teas, and outlet stores. A rodeo was coming to the area. Callie picked that one up and quickly put it back; the event had been and gone a month ago.

Maybe she'd go for a drive to admire the views of the fall foliage and stop at an apple orchard. Then, she noticed a brochure for an apple orchard jammed crookedly in one of the slots. Callie picked the misplaced advertisement out of the wrong slot and put it back where it belonged in the compartment for Big Apple Friendly Farms.

Disorganization bothered her. People at her job teased her about her penchant for order but their teasing didn't bother her. What bothered her was being *disorganized* with all the problems *that* could cause. As a white hat hacker and analyst, she knew from experience the benefits of being meticulous.

New York Renaissance Festival was emblazoned in bright yellow letters on the brochures that were revealed. A medieval-looking knight in shining armor was front and center. His jousting stick? pole?--she couldn't think of the right name--pointed at the camera. Oval snapshots of lords and ladies, wenches and peasants, tankards of drinks and giant turkey legs adorned the rest of the cover. "From now until mid-October" was displayed at the bottom of the page.

Callie unfolded the glossy paper to make sure it was from the current year. Even though it was still September, it wouldn't help to find out that this was from two years ago. It was current. She refolded the glossy paper and tucked it into the front flap of her crossbody bag along with a couple for apple orchards and one about the tea parlor.

It was hard to turn off the work- focused part of her brain.

She left the alcove with the maps and display rack and crossed the space with the welcome desk and a seating area. Melody wasn't at the front desk. A plump woman in a cardigan with a name tag that identified her as Mrs. Wheeler was busily turning the pages of a ledger, but she immediately refocused her attention on Callie. "Settling in okay, Ms. Stewart?"

"Everything is great. Really."

Except I don't want to be here. And how do you know my name?

Mrs. Wheeler beamed. "Melody said you are a good sort, and she's never wrong about those things."

Unsure how to respond to that comment, Callie smiled and said, "I was looking at some of the area attractions."

"Anything catch your fancy?"

"How is the Renaissance Festival?"

Mrs. Wheeler seemed somehow even cheerier. "That's my favorite event all year, except maybe for the Christmas Festival. It's right up there with AppleFest."

Callie didn't know when AppleFest was, and she wasn't sure she wanted to know. "Well, that's a good endorsement," she said. "The schedule says it's open Thursday through Sunday this week."

"You'll probably want to go today, unless you have other things planned already. It's the least crowded day, and then you can go back again if you love it," Mrs. Wheeler said.

"The ticket is a little pricey. But you think it's worth it?"

"*Everybody* loves it." The older woman leaned across the desk and lowered her voice. "Make sure you go to the Joust! They do it a few times every day. I swear, they find the hottest men to participate in that. You wouldn't think suits of armor would be sexy but whew..." Mrs. Wheeler waggled her eyebrows dramatically and fanned her face with her hand.

Callie couldn't help but laugh at the woman describing men as "hot" and "sexy," and Mrs. Wheeler laughed right along with her. "My eyes still work fine, don't you know."

Chapter 3

Callie

After three hours at the Renaissance Festival, Callie was annoyed that she'd never been to it before. Annoyed and surprised. The headquarters of the company she worked for were on Long Island, only a few hours away. She'd grown up in Virginia, not far from D.C., and knew a lot about the eastern seaboard. So how had she never known about this annual, months-long event?

The raucous festival was a surreal mix of medieval and modern. Renaissance Festival employees in lavish costumes mixed with visitors in their own versions of medieval garb, and both versions of the upper-class people were set apart by those in peasant clothing and modern, contemporary attire. After a little while, seeing costumed courtiers next to contemporary tourist clothing seemed... normal. There was almost too much to look at. Musicians strolled the grounds alone and in small groups, strumming guitars and old-fashioned stringed instruments or blowing through wind instruments that looked like they were right out of a history book. Or off a movie set.

Callie's stomach rumbled. Oh, this place smelled so good! The aroma of roasting meats filled the air. Steaks, hamburgers, sausages, and chicken tenders were sold alongside rustic bowls of stew and platters of vegetables. There were even giant turkey legs like she'd seen in the brochure she snagged at the B&B. Water and soft drinks were everywhere. Barmaids served up ale, mead, and beer.

Callie tossed her empty lemonade cup into the side opening of a covered trash bin cleverly disguised as a tree stump. Breakfast was a distant memory already, and her stomach again announced its displeasure. Time to find a restroom, then grab food and a cup of ale. She consulted her paper map of the huge festival grounds, trying to figure out her location. A shadow fell across her face and upon the map in her hands.

"Have ye lost your way, my lady?" A man's deep, resonant voice threw a shiver down her spine.

Callie looked up at the owner of that voice, and again felt like she'd somehow wandered onto a movie set. He was the epitome of a ruggedly handsome hero, with dark, wavy hair, silvery gray eyes, and a sculpted jaw blanketed by a closely cropped beard.

"Just checking my map," she said awkwardly. She didn't want to tell the fine specimen of a man in front of her that she was looking for a place to pee.

"If perchance ye seek a room in which to rest, there is one a few hundred yards yonder." The sunshine didn't seem to bother his eyes, which were steadily fixed on her.

"Thanks. Do you work here?" She gestured at his linen shirt with the laces at the neck and his snug-fitting trousers, both in shades of brown. He wore a black vest with lavish details stitched onto it, a wide leather belt, and knee-high black boots. Was he an employee, or simply an enthusiastic fan of the Renaissance Festival?

The man arched a dark eyebrow and looked down at her from what had to be at least seven inches above her 5'5" height. "*Work?*" His tone made clear his character felt abject horror at the thought. "My lady, I am here to joust, as a noble man does. Not to work."

He sneered as he said the last word. It was done so effectively that she couldn't *not* smile. He met her smile with a brilliant but fleeting one of his own.

Then his eyes shifted to something or someone over her shoulder.

"Forgive my hasty departure, but I must go." The man sketched a hasty bow to Callie and took off diagonally across the square in which they stood. In moments he'd disappeared among the crowds.

Callie stared in the direction the mystery man had gone. Why had he rushed off like that? She knew part of the job of working the Renaissance Festival involved interacting with the public, and surely rudeness wasn't part of that.

Who did he spot in the crowd? She wasn't certain, but it seemed he'd gone in a different direction from whatever or whoever had caught his attention. Maybe his girlfriend or his wife, and he didn't want her seeing him doing his job? Maybe just a sexy visitor to the fair, and the appeal of chatting her up was too much to resist?

No way a guy who looked like *him* was available, or if somehow he was, that he would be interested in *her*. Not at all. He was just talking to her as part of the overall experience of attending the festival.

Still... Callie kept thinking as she resumed walking. Her sixth sense of something not being right, or of it being more important than it seemed to be on the face of it, usually served her well at her job. That disquieting feeling was strong right now. Call it a gut instinct, intuition, or a hunch.

Whatever that foreboding was this time, Callie tried to shake it off. She needed to relax. Sternly, she reminded herself she wasn't working on a case.

Callie had six more days of this vacation she hadn't wanted to take, and she needed to try and make the most of it. There were plenty of entertainment options at the festival that she hadn't explored yet.

Callie allowed herself to be drawn toward one of the marketplace areas. She could probably also find excellent souvenirs among all the merchant stalls. From the size of the crowds swarming them, there had to be some worthwhile things to be found.

Chapter 4

Lance

Lance checked the phone in his trouser pocket. Some things about working for the Renaissance Festival were actually cool and even fun. The huge list of rules wasn't. One of strictest rules was the ban on anything anachronistic to the historical "time." For festival purposes, that time period spanned a couple hundred years, so it wasn't accurate either. Regardless, it was blatantly against the rules for festival staff to reveal tech on their persons, but screw that; he had to know the exact time.

After seeing the time, Lance increased his pace until he was nearly jogging. His brief conversation with that woman had delayed him more than he'd realized. He shouldn't have started an interaction with her, but he'd done so before he'd really thought about it. Now he was risking being late. His meetings with his contact were never spaced so close together, but the guy had signaled there were urgent circumstances.

Eckert better be on time, and it better be important. Lance was cutting it too close to when he needed to change into his modified suit of armor for the joust. That role was a key part of his cover persona, and he couldn't risk jeopardizing it.

Moving with confidence, Lance ducked behind a trio of frozen beverage vendors. Took care where he placed his booted feet when he made his way around the labyrinth of electrical wires and power cords. This time he went a bit further north, passing behind the comfort station and into the forest area adjacent to the Section D supply buildings where Eckert was already waiting. The thin man's agitation was obvious by how much he was sweating, and by how rapidly a muscle by his eyelid kept twitching.

"He knows." Eckert shifted from one foot to the other and back again. "I'm out." He licked his lips and repeated, "I'm out."

Lance focused on Eckert's first statement. "How do *you* know that?"

"I'm being followed," Eckert said. His eyes kept darting around the trees, apparently on the lookout for whoever he thought was following him.

"You're sure?" Lance pressed. "Talk to me. Who's following you?"

"Yeah." Eckert nodded. "Sometimes a guy. Sometimes a woman. All the time."

"Today. Who's following you today?"

"Yeah, today. A woman." His informant ran both hands through his already disheveled blonde hair. "I gotta go."

Eckert turned to do exactly that.

"Wait." Lance said quietly, but the command was clear. "What do you have for me?"

"Nothing. I told you I'm out."

"This doesn't work that way."

"Fuck you. And don't try to find me. It's not worth dying for this." Heedless of the noise he caused, Eckert took off into the woods.

Lance wanted to run after him and get more info about what spooked the man so badly, but he didn't have time. Maintaining his cover was vital to the mission. Right now, that meant he had to be on time for the joust. He turned to head back the way he'd come.

Through a gap between the trees a woman had eyes on him. A

beautiful woman. The woman who'd spoken to him when he was on his way to meet Eckert. Was she the woman following his informant?

"You!" Lance called out, running towards her. "Don't go anywhere."

She turned on her heel and took off.

Chapter 5

Callie

What the hell was that about?

Following him hadn't been easy after he took off the way he did, but she'd been compelled to try. More than once she'd made a directional decision purely based on instinct.

There's that word again.

When she found him, the Renaissance Festival man was in tense conversation with a guy whose body language positively screamed tension and agitation, and who literally ran away. Before he shuttered his expression, Callie could see that Renaissance man was furious.

He shouted at her to stop, but no way was she doing that, especially when she had no idea what was going on. Instead, she took off in another direction into the trees.

She'd been right; something strange was going on.

Callie stopped running fairly quickly, not wanting to attract attention to herself. She joined a group of people waiting to buy hot pretzels from a vendor. While she nibbled at the buttery treat wrapped in wax paper, she maintained an eye on her surroundings and considered what to do next.

The last joust of the day was coming up soon, according to the events board she could see posted in the nearest square. The mystery man had mentioned getting ready for the joust. He could've just been saying that, of course, but maybe he really was a participant? It was an event she wanted to see anyway, and now she had an additional reason to be interested. Otherwise, she could just wander around the fairgrounds and see if she spotted him anywhere, or she could continue looking at souvenirs. Maybe she could catch a couple of the smaller acts in different areas. Maybe she could simply relax. She was on her vacation.

Callie's feet were carrying her in the direction she needed to go before she even acknowledged that she'd made her choice. There were numerous signs pointing in the direction of the jousting field, and the closer she got the more groups of people were streaming in that direction.

Callie scoped out the grandstands at the large jousting field. There were many areas for people to stand and watch the proceedings. The area was particularly loud, the crowd boisterous. People were talking, musicians playing, vendors hawking items in modern takes on Olde English vernacular. The crowds had been basically enthusiastic all day, but for this event, there was a whole other level of excitement.

As trumpeters and pipers heralded the beginning of the event, a procession of costumed spectators made their way into a sectioned-off area at the front of the spectator section. Among them, tall banners with coats of arms apparently indicated positions and titles of "honored guests."

A drumroll sounded from somewhere, and an elegant woman on horseback with elaborately layered gowns draped over the back of her mount galloped into the ring. In a clear voice, she welcomed spectators to the joust.

There would be four competitors. Each was introduced and took a turn galloping their respective horses along straight tracks delineated by wooden barriers. As each made that introductory run, they also practiced their aim with the lances they carried. Each knight was assigned a quadrant of spectators as their cheering squad. Everyone who was amassed to watch the event quickly became engaged in the excitement.

Sir William. Sir Stephen. The White Knight. The Dark Knight. Callie didn't recognize any of the first three Knights. Each was dressed in medieval garb topped with different degrees of chain mail or metal armor. The fourth competitor, the Dark Knight, had a lowered faceplate that hid his features. The man she'd spoken to earlier had said he was in the joust, so by process of elimination, if he'd made that claim truthfully, he was the Dark Knight.

As the competition progressed, the Knights moved through different types of weapons, different types of combat. Although she wasn't a field operative, because of her line of work, Callie herself had been trained with modern knives and modern combat techniques. She found herself enthralled in the action on the field – and even more enthralled by the imposing figure of the Dark Knight.

The Dark Knight flung away his helmet and another man costumed as his assistant divested him of his armor. His eyes met hers immediately; Callie realized he must've noticed her while he'd still worn the faceplate. Otherwise, he wouldn't have located her so quickly.

The man had been graceful on horseback even under the weight of his armor. Somehow, without it, he appeared even more imposing. Many of the men she worked with were attractive. But none of them made her blood run hotly the way this man did. When they first spoken, she'd felt that initial buzz of attraction. When she saw him through the trees in confrontation with the blonde man, physical distance hadn't hidden his controlled energy. Now, it was obvious to Callie's eyes that he was a trained fighter in real life, not just trained in performance choreography for the jousting show.

Why was he here? What had been going on during that tense

conversation she'd seen between him and that other man? Why did she have that feeling of foreboding around him?

She wasn't on assignment. This didn't involve White Hat hacking, code breaking, or any of her usual skill set. But she damn well wasn't going to ignore her instincts.

Vacation or not, she was going to find out.

Chapter 6

Lance

Lance didn't believe for a second that the woman he'd seen spying on him and Eckert in the woods *just happened* to be the one he'd spoken to earlier, and then *just happened* to be at the joust. In his section. From the way her eyes assessed him, she appeared to be evaluating his fighting skills and his form. Damn Eckert for taking off so quickly! Was she the woman who'd been tailing his informant?

Lance reminded himself that he was working. That her warm brown eyes with their startlingly long lashes, lush mahogany hair with its auburn highlights, and full lips could not be a distraction. Neither could her graceful body with its enticing curves. He needed to focus on the joust and, more importantly, on his bigger purpose. Criminals using the festival as a cover for their activities wasn't only illegal; it was also dangerous for the innocent people in attendance.

If she was connected to that, he would know soon enough.

Hopefully, she wasn't.

Earlier, when he shouted at her to stay, she'd ignored him. But now she wasn't fleeing the jousting field. As soon he was free of his character's armor, he handed it off to someone from costuming who was dressed as a page.

Lance headed in the mystery woman's direction. The area always emptied slowly after a jousting show, with spectators taking photos of the participants, and with them when possible. He pasted on a small smile but avoided making direct eye contact with anyone else. The mystery woman held his gaze steadily as he approached her.

Lance stayed a respectful distance so he wouldn't crowd her space, and asked, "Did you enjoy the show?"

Her answering smile came across as genuine. "I did. The joust was exciting, and you were terrific."

"I'm glad you enjoyed it." He sent her what he hoped was a charming smile. "I'm done for the day. I have to confess that jousting is hungry work. Can I interest you in having dinner with me? Maybe we could go somewhere that isn't here."

"We've shared a whole two minutes of conversation. That's how fast you invite a woman you've never met before to dinner?"

He gestured at their surroundings. "It appears we have some things, some interests, in common."

"Both of us being at the Renaissance Festival isn't necessarily common ground. There's a big difference between jousting and souvenir shopping."

"True, but I know shopping can be pretty dangerous here when it gets crowded." Lance pretended to cringe in horror, then said, "There *is* more than that. We're both here on the same day."

She smiled and shook her head. "Coincidence isn't common ground."

Lance shrugged. "We've run into each other three times today."

"Again, coincidence."

He leaned in toward her conspiratorially. "Let me put it this way. I strongly suspect we have much in common."

"You do, do you?" She hesitated, and Lance could see the indecision on her expressive face. She wanted to accept his invitation. Either she was actually just a visitor to the festival and uncertain of his intentions, or she was up to no good and had another agenda. An agenda she might be trying to figure out how he could benefit.

"Look," he said before she could potentially refuse him, "there are some excellent local restaurants I've been to around here. You could follow me in your own vehicle if you have one with you, that is. Or are you with a group?"

"I do have a car," she said. "There's another problem with your invitation, though."

"We haven't yet been introduced," he said, as if confident that was going to be her next point. He tried to level-up on the charm. God, he hated this; it was why the taciturn character of the Dark Knight suited him. "Fortunately for us, this isn't really the Middle Ages, and we don't have to find someone else to introduce us." He extended his hand. "Lance Mulholland."

No way was he giving her his real last name.

She shook his hand, and he heard her trying to smother her laugh. "Lance, like in Lancelot?"

"No. That would be ironic, though, right?"

"It would be a casting director's dream. I'm Callie," she said, and shook his hand. Her hand was small within his own, and her handshake was confident. "Callie Conway."

"It's a pleasure to meet you, Callie Conway. Can I interest you in dinner with me tonight, as a regular guy, not a knight in shining armor?"

"Yes, I think I'd like that."

Chapter 7

Callie

Not quite an hour later, Callie sat across from Lance at a table for two at Fiona's Kitchen, studying him in the light from the tabletop candle. The restaurant was quiet and calm, a perfect counterpoint to the chaotic atmosphere of the Renaissance Festival.

"The food is good here," Lance said. "It's a nice place to come and wind down after a long day spent at the fairgrounds." He leaned back in his chair. "Being here with you only makes it better."

Lance was smooth, all right. Charming. Well-spoken. Easygoing. He was also hiding something. Her gut was sure of it.

It figured, right?

Callie studied the laminated restaurant menu. Lots of straightforward, simple choices, all of which sounded appealing. She looked at him over the top edge. "Do you recommend anything in particular?"

"Personally, I think you can't go wrong with a burger, the chicken pot pie, or the Irish stew. I've ordered each of those multiple times, and they're always good."

She nodded, making a sound of approval. Was Lance in the habit of picking up women at the festival and bringing them here? Maybe he was a player and that's what she was sensing.

Well, whatever was setting her internal alarm bells off, *something* was doing it. So no romantic fling was in the cards for her vacation, but she could figure out what Lance Mulholland was up to. What he was hiding.

"May I take your order?" The waitress returned to their table with their drinks, diet soda for Callie and iced tea for Lance. The woman tucked her small round tray under one arm and pulled a notepad and pencil from her apron pocket. "Are you ready to order, or do you have any questions about the menu?"

"Ladies first," Lance said. "Callie?"

It took less than two minutes for her to order a burger with fries, and Lance to do the same. The server left to put in their order, and quiet descended on the table.

Maybe Lance was simply some kind of creep? She immediately shut down that thought as doubtful. Her instincts were somehow always good about character, and she wasn't getting that kind of vibe from him. He didn't even seem shady. More like... secretive.

Maybe he's married? It wouldn't be the first time a guy in a monogamous relationship had pretended to be single for his own selfish purposes. She wasn't getting burned like that again, but she really didn't think that was it either.

Callie broke the silence. "You said you're staying in a nearby hotel. In town?"

"Right next to the turnoff for the festival," he said. "My pay is decent, but not enough to waste a lot on a fancy place for two months." He sipped his iced tea. "The festival season drives up prices. There are a couple of big chain hotels about half hour or more down the mountain, the kinds that have reward programs and concierge levels. Motels in the area offer discounts to festival workers, so that was an easy decision."

It was equally easy to hide her fishing expedition when Callie was genuinely curious. "Do most people who work at the festival live locally? If not, it's got to be hard for everyone to rent for the whole season."

"Some do, some don't," Lance said. "Specialty acts, unique foods, merchants with wares specific to the time, they all mostly travel the circuit. If you're on the circuit you see some of the same people on repeat, in different states, different towns." He changed the subject. "How long are you in town? Are you just here for the festival?"

"Not long." Callie followed up what she knew was a vague answer with another question of her own. "What's your regular job?"

"You don't think I'm a joust professional?" Lance smirked, accentuating his lighthearted comment. "Nothing exciting. I teach riding sometimes. Mostly in the Midwest."

The arrival of their burgers interrupted conversation as the hot plates were set on the table. Despite her interest in getting more info, Callie was glad to see Lance was right about his recommendation of the restaurant. The food looked and smelled delicious.

After several minutes of them both enthusiastically enjoying the casual meals in front of them, she returned to the conversation they'd been having before the platters arrived.

"What do you leave behind when you travel for the Renaissance festivals? No Guinevere sitting at home in the castle and missing you?" Callie probed, genuinely curious.

If he really was on the up-and-up, how likely was it that he was truly single? Maybe her instincts were wrong. Otherwise, what was she sensing about him that had her on high alert?

"If there was someone waiting anywhere for me, I wouldn't be having dinner with you," he said seriously. "The Lancelot in the legend of King Arthur may have had an affair with the married Guinevere, but that's certainly nothing I would ever do. I'd never interfere in someone's relationship, or disrespect one of my own."

An awkward silence settled between them after that remark. She tried to direct the conversation back into lighter territory. "I meant no offense," she said. "So, the Dark Knight is really a good guy after all. Better not let people know that or it might ruin your brand."

"At least in some ways, I guess," he said, then redirected the conversation back to her. "What kind of work do you do, Callie?"

"Marketing and promotion," she answered smoothly. It was a good cover, neatly explaining her high-end computers and anything related to them. Not that Lance knew about those, but still...

Callie wanted to get more information about this guy. Not like she could invite him back to the B&B to do a soft interrogation. Well, technically, she could. It was certainly a benefit of having a little cabin all to herself.

She tried to remember if there was anything left visible in her space there that would reveal her actual employer, or her last name. She didn't think so, but she wasn't 100% sure. It would be a risk.

Her female friends at Infinite Security had encouraged her to have a wild vacation, but going back to this guy's place tonight – that would be bordering on foolish. No one would know who she was with, or where she was. Since she had that nagging feeling that something was off about him, it would be stupid to put herself in potential trouble. Potential danger.

Instead, she asked, "Are you working tomorrow?"

"Yes. It's a short season, not a lot of days off." Lance wiped his mouth with the green cloth napkin and dropped it back onto his lap.

"I might go to the festival again, but I'm not sure yet." Callie didn't have to feign nervousness at the question she was going to ask. She was all for female empowerment, but still never felt comfortable asking a man for a date. Even a date that would also be business – at least on her side. "Do you happen to have dinner plans tomorrow?"

His slow smile pleased her. "I do now."

Chapter 8

Lance

Several hours after he said goodbye to Callie outside Fiona's Kitchen, Lance was sure that Callie Conway didn't exist. He did a basic Internet search for every variation he could think of for her first and last names. What could Callie stand for? Colleen. Caroline. Calista. Nothing that could be the woman he met at the festival.

He uploaded the three images he'd covertly snapped of her and sent them to Daughtry in an encrypted file. Hopefully, she'd pop up in a database search utilizing facial recognition software. The license plate on her vehicle revealed it to be a rental. If need be, they'd try to pinpoint the rental agency and access those records.

He left his shoes just inside the door of his room. Then Lance pulled off his lightweight sweater and tossed it on the chair. He needed a shower to wash off the exertions of a long day. He padded into the bathroom, phone in hand. If he received a call back, he didn't want to miss it.

It'd been simple enough to shadow Callie back to the B&B where she was staying. He hadn't known if her room was in the main house there, or in one of the outbuildings. He didn't ask over dinner because he didn't want to appear to be a creeper or have her realize he was investigating her. Easier to pull that info directly from the B&B's own records. Even easier to watch with his own eyes as the taillights of her car disappeared down the winding private road that led to the outbuildings of the B&B.

Lance finished stripping in the utilitarian bathroom. This economy motel was fine for his purposes, and he hadn't lied when he'd explained its benefits to Callie. *If that was really her name.* But it'd be nice to get back to showering with better water pressure.

His lips twisted slightly into something that resembled a self-deprecating smile. His years in the service had gotten him accustomed to appreciating any chance to get clean, even when under a hanging water back. But several years in the private sector already had him spoiled. Lance set his phone on the narrow bathroom counter. He stepped into the shower, which was perfectly clean and acceptable, despite the unreliable water pressure.

Could Callie really be part of the ring stealing and dealing artifacts through the Renaissance Festival? She didn't look like someone with a particular interest in medieval and similar weaponry or jewelry. He'd learned, though, that the players in the underground antiquities market weren't always what one might imagine them to be-- especially since the money was being used to fund terrorists.

In the decades since September 11 rocked America, people had become complacent. Homeland Security and the alphabet soup agencies tasked with tracking and intercepting terrorist activity were almost shockingly successful. So much so that people could go about their daily lives, their daily business, without interruption from the shadowy forces that lurked under the surface in too many places.

Lance rinsed the soap from his hair and started scrubbing down his skin. Modern tactical gear wasn't lightweight and comfortable, when compared to casual clothing. But it was a wonder of safety innovations compared to what had gone before – especially suits of armor. Even the adapted replicas he wore at the festival were damn uncomfortable.

He finished his perfunctory shower, his mind still on the job he was really doing at the festival.

Lance hated knowing that no matter how many murderous plots and insidious funding streams were stopped, more were always sliding into position to take their place. Money truly made the world go around. Judges and government officials on the take, business people willing to make deals under the table, there were a lot of individuals in key positions willing to look the other way in exchange for lavish gifts, well-placed bribes, and thick envelopes stuffed with cash.

Lance shook his head at his own cynical thoughts; he knew better than most that you couldn't judge someone based on outer appearance. After all, he wasn't what he appeared to be either.

Eckert said a woman was following him. Callie, or whatever her name was, had appeared at the periphery of their meeting as if right on cue. Sure, her appearance could have been a coincidence. Except for the fact that true coincidences were about as rare as snowstorms in August.

He'd keep looking, but Daughtry would probably get faster results with the resources at headquarters.

Damn shame such a sexy woman might be a criminal. Was she also a terrorist sympathizer, or was she a common thief?

Chapter 9

Callie

Wrapped in a plush robe provided by the B&B, Callie quickly set up a secure connection on the primary laptop she traveled with. In its disaster -proof, decoy case it didn't even look like a computer, but that was a benefit because it also didn't attract attention as something worth stealing.

She linked to Infinite Security via a secure VPN and followed the necessary steps to access one of the databases she wanted to use. Focused on her goal, Callie started searching for Lance Mulholland. As she was trying every possible permutation of his name, a chat screen message popped up from Rick.

"You're on vacation," her direct boss wrote. "Why are you searching for someone? Is he a potential dinner date?"

Wise ass.

"I already had dinner with him," she typed back. "I don't know what it is, but something isn't right with this guy."

It wasn't a surprise when her phone rang.

The concern in Rick's voice was unmistakable. "What do you mean by not right? What did he do? Are you okay?"

"He didn't do anything to *me*," Callie said.

"Callie, talk to me." She could picture the serious expression on Rick's face.

She took her hands off the keyboard and settled back in the chair. "I observed a tense conversation in a strange place between two guys acting suspiciously. I got the name of one of them, spent a little time with him, but can't find any info on him. "

"You're leaving out a lot of information here. Where did this happen? What were they talking about?"

"At the Renaissance Festival. I couldn't hear them."

Rick fired several questions in quick succession. "How do you know it was a tense conversation? Why was it a strange place? I mean, sure there are some strange people at those things, but isn't that part of the fun? How are they acting suspiciously?"

Callie reminded herself that from his perspective, it had to sound strange. "Body language, Rick. Body language is the answer to questions one and four. And it was strange because they were in a remote corner of the fairgrounds. Like they didn't want anyone to overhear them."

"Callie, I'm just not getting this. Why are you so interested in something two guys were talking about privately at a Renaissance fair?" Rick didn't sound like he was teasing, more like he was genuinely perplexed.

"I can't explain it better than I just did. Something was off about it all." She could look into this for herself, but it would definitely be easier if someone was helping from the office.

While she spoke, Callie could hear the sounds of Rick typing quickly on a keyboard. "You typed this in your search, but if you tell me it'll be quicker. Name?"

"Lance Mulholland," she said. "I can send a couple pictures I took of him at the Renaissance Festival today. He is a performer there." Callie paused. "I also may have swiped his silverware at dinner last night to grab his fingerprints."

"You're that suspicious about this guy?" Rick said. "But you had dinner with him."

This wasn't a company investigation. She was on her own time, and didn't feel like she had to explain herself. But she kind of did because Rick was helping her. "It was a casual dinner in a public place. It's not like I went off somewhere secluded with him."

"What does he do at the festival? Why do you think he's up to something?"

"People who work at the Renaissance Festival are part of a of cast of characters. The name of Lance's his character is the Dark Knight. . He portrays exactly what it sounds like, a Renaissance era knight." Callie made a face. She could imagine the jokes that were about to begin. There was a moment of silence.

Rick said, "And his name is Lance?"

"That's what he said."

Over the phone, she heard the familiar sounds of fingers striking a keyboard. "I was just looking up the festival. Let me wrap my head around this. He's a participant in the medieval jousts. He carries a lance, and his name is . . . *Lance*."

"Are you done?" Callie sighed.

"He doesn't sound like an arch-criminal, and he's not very creative with his naming skills." Rick paused his typing. "How old do you think he is? Coloring?"

"I'd say he's mid to late-30s. Dark hair, gray eyes."

"Send the pictures to my phone, and I'll see what I can find from here. Keep the other items secure until you can get them here." He paused. "Or are you going to lift the prints yourself?"

"No, I don't have supplies for that. I'm hoping the pictures give us some info."

If there was something to be found, Rick would find it. He had more resources back at headquarters than she had on one laptop.

Callie looked again at the images she'd sent to her coworker. It figured that the hottest guy she'd met in ages would be a criminal.

Chapter 10

Callie

Parking spaces near the entrance of the Renaissance Festival were extremely limited. There was parking for visitors with disabilities, and drop-off lanes for tour buses, school buses, camp buses, senior center buses, and other groups of people visiting en masse. The regular parking fields were further down and across the road. The event provided shuttle service from those lots, and foot paths for those who wanted to walk.

As Callie emerged from one of the crowded shuttle buses, she inhaled the fresh morning air. The gates opened at 10 o'clock in the morning, and it was only 11 o'clock. Medieval heralds in short pantaloons and half-cloaks stood at attention on both sides of the wooden gates that led to the fairgrounds. Their fanfares, music, and shouts punctuated the stillness and increase the anticipation of those still waiting to purchase their tickets and join the fun.

Apparently, every day was a party at the Renaissance Festival.

Once through the entrance gates, the knot of people gradually dispersed. The layout was skillfully designed to coax people in a variety of directions. Wooden signposts and a carved map offered guidance; food, beverages, restrooms, merchants, hair braiding, face painting, body piercing, petting zoo, horse stables, mud pit, chess field, music... The options went on and on. Another board listed showtimes for specific acts and events, including the joust.

Callie hesitated, unsure where to look for Lance; she didn't even know if he was there yet, just that he was working at some point today. Over dinner, he'd mentioned that part of his duties involved interacting with crowds, but he hadn't gone into much more detail about that.

She meandered through food stalls and alternated between looking at what was for sale and who was milling about or buying things for themselves. Breakfast at the B&B had been delicious and filling again today, but the enticing aromas of the foods for sale still competed for her attention.

"Good morning." Lance was speaking to her before she had a chance to recognize that the prickling of the skin at the back of her neck signaled that he was there.

Callie was top-notch at electronic surveillance, but she was also no slouch at core field skills involving real-time, in-person observation and situational awareness. Except, apparently, she was worse than a slouch today. How had she not seen him making his way toward her? Had she really sensed his presence without knowing what it was?

Several women were jostling each other, literally falling over themselves trying to get his attention or snap a picture with him. Not that it mattered to her, but their attention was ridiculous – like he was some kind of rock star who unexpectedly showed up in a local bar on a Saturday night.

When he had her attention, Lance bowed in her direction. "A pleasure to see you again, milady."

Callie wasn't going to be distracted by his handsome face or the impressive sight he was in his snug black pants tucked into tall boots and a closely fitted black shirt with the cord lacing open at the neck.

She steeled herself against the wave of physical attraction that washed over her and said, "We need to have a private conversation."

"Good idea." Lance bowed slightly to the rest of the women clustered about, then gripped her elbow more firmly than was really necessary. "Let's do that, shall we?"

The audible sounds of disappointment at his departure followed them when he guided her away from the group. She didn't speak as he led her out of the main area and toward one of the narrower paths that branched off to the right. Several people greeted him as they passed by, and Callie saw multiple phones angled in his direction. Lance directed a curt nod to some people, a raised eyebrow or a scowl to others. From what she could see as they moved along, visitors were pleased with his unfriendly reactions.

"They like when you're cold and obnoxious to them?" It made no sense to her.

He glanced down at her. "Of course they do. The Dark Knight isn't a warm and caring guy."

Of course. She hadn't thought of it that way. Lance wasn't simply a man working at the fair, but a character in what was, essentially, a huge theater production. Callie *knew* that, even mentioned it to Rick last night, but she hadn't really thought about what that meant. Was her suspicion that he was hiding something simply her picking up on the fact that he was hiding his *real* personality behind the façade of the character he was portraying?

Hand-painted signage on the pathway indicated it led to the "Living Chessboard" area, and that the show wouldn't be for several hours yet. Yesterday, she'd noticed the attraction mentioned in her brochure, but she hadn't the time to check it out.

The sounds and scents of the festival faded significantly the further they walked. Lance finally stopped in the center of a large clearing. To the left of the area was a giant checkerboard, roped-off to keep people from walking on it. There were two people on the other side of the board, in peasant attire, comparing notes on clipboards. One of them acknowledged Lance with a chin lift, but aside from that, the staff members ignored them.

Lance faced her directly and with no preamble asked, "Who are you, really?"

Callie wasn't expecting that question, but she countered without hesitation. "I was going to ask you the same thing. Who are you? Honestly."

"I told you who I am," he said. His eyes were cold, unlike at dinner last night. They looked like steel marbles, his gaze assessing.

She'd been wary before, but now she was angry. He was up to no good, she was sure of it, and she didn't appreciate him trying to make her out to be the one in the wrong. Callie consciously kept her voice down as she snapped out her response.

"You gave me what might be your first name and a fake surname. Right now, as we speak, your fingerprints are being run." *Well, they will be soon.* "We'll have your identity confirmed soon enough," she said. "I'm giving you a chance to come clean before I alert the authorities."

Did he know she was bluffing?

"Nice try," he said. "What about me could possibly interest the local authority? Part of my job is acting. I use a stage name. Not a crime." He took a step closer. "What's your excuse?"

"You're giving *me* grief because I gave a complete stranger a fake name?" Callie rolled her eyes. "Safety 101, especially for women."

They stood there, toe to toe, cloaked in silence. Even though they were outdoors, Lance's presence filled the space around and between them. He folded his arms and shifted into a sexy lean against a slim tree trunk. But he didn't speak again, merely observed her with narrowed eyes. The heat in his lingering gaze matched the fire he'd lit inside her already. At work, her ability to focus never failed her, but with this man she couldn't stop wondering how his lips would feel on hers. How his –

Callie broke the silent standoff and put the brake on her loud train of thoughts. "*My* people are aware I'm speaking to you now. If I don't check in at the appointed time, my backup will be all over this place."

"Backup from Infinite Security?" Lance crossed his arms over his broad chest. "Yeah, I know a lot about *you* already, Callie." He tilted his head to one side and narrowed his eyes. "I also know people at your company."

They were both using secret identities? Or a stage name for him and caution for them both? Pieces quickly slotted into place, and she realized he was with another agency, investigating... something.

Callie changed her approach. "Who do you work for? What exactly are you doing here?"

Lance was quiet so long she thought he was refusing to answer. Then he said, "Guardian Force. Stolen antiquities."

Guardian Force was a security agency she'd heard of, although it was smaller than Infinite. She heard somebody at work mentioning it a couple of times, but she would have to think about it to remember who it was.

Callie thought the "something" he might be there for would have to do with drugs. Guns. Trafficking. Antiquities had never crossed her mind.

Chapter 11

Lance

It'd been ridiculously easy to find out Callie's real last name and the company she worked for. Easy for *him*, at least. And he'd seen her swipe his silverware under the guise of stumbling against the table upon their departure from the restaurant.

The B&B's simple reservation system was easy to hack; he would have done it the first night and he realized getting information about her would be important. She was checked in at the B&B under her real name, obviously never thinking that she might need or want to hide her identity on her vacation. Who would?

Her vehicle was rented by a shell corporation within another shell corporation. Then he got a huge break; an executive of that company was a name he recognized from his Army Ranger days. Hell, his friend Jace even tried to recruit him to Infinite Security a year ago, but Lance's contract at Guardian wasn't up yet.

Lance could tell her what was going on. Maybe she could even help him bring it to a close. Maybe.

"Here's the short version," Lance said. "You saw all the vendors of medieval style merchandise?" When Callie nodded, he continued. "Two have been selling authentic merchandise alongside reproduction items. The authentic things go to only specific, repeat buyers. The purchasers pay an amount in keeping with a good reproduction and slip the vendor a sealed package that contains a lot of cash."

"Right out in the open?"

Loud voices carried on the breeze as a bigger crew of Festival workers arrived at the site to continue set up for the day's living chess match. He slipped an arm around Callie's waist as an excuse to pull her closer and lowered his voice even more. "It's slick, but yes, right at the booth in the middle of the regular transactions."

Callie's gaze searched his face, as if looking for the answers to the questions she asked, "Why? What's the endgame?"

"We think the real sellers are dealers in stolen or otherwise illegally obtained antique weapons, decorative items, jewelry, things like that. The two involved here are middlemen who don't even open the sealed packages." Lance looked around them again, then spoke directly against her ear. "I've tracked them to see packets handed off in the parking fields."

"If this is a big op, why are you working alone?" she demanded. "That doesn't make any sense."

He couldn't fault her for asking that; it didn't make sense. And it hadn't started out that way. "My partner broke his ankle while working undercover here as a performer. The other person working within the Festival was pulled because a more critical case needed his particular expertise. I have additional back-up working in the parking lots and ticketing."

Lance gripped the back of his neck in frustration. "It's difficult to have someone join the cast of performers during the season, or even join the overall crew. It pays well, all things considered, and people don't just quit. We can't hurt someone or randomly force anybody out to make a job opening."

Callie asked a logical question. "Someone in management must know what's going on. Can't a new job opening be created?"

"The answers to both those questions are more complicated than you might think. The bottom line is . . . *no.*"

Callie seemed to speak thoughtfully, now watching some of the cleverly attired chess pieces arriving to the clearing. "This festival is only a couple months a year, right? What do these antiquities dealers do during the rest of the year?"

"There are other Renaissance Festivals and other organizations around the country that have similar events with similar vendors."

"The bad guys always find a way," she said.

Lance watched along with her as more staff arrived. Damn, he felt a wash of sympathy for the Bishop, King, and Queen chess pieces. Their costumes looked miserably heavy and uncomfortable. He preferred dealing with his suit of armor. He could hear the sounds of excited Festival attendees lining up behind the ropes.

Watching them, his focus was still on Callie. "The man you saw me talking to yesterday, he was giving me information about movements of people of interest."

"To me, he looked like he wanted out of whatever situation he was in," Callie said. "He couldn't wait to get away from you."

"It was *you* he couldn't wait to get away from." Bracing his hands on his hips, Lance corrected her. "He said a blonde woman in a baseball cap was following him. I was scanning the perimeter, looked to the left again, and saw you."

"Spying from the bushes."

Lance nodded. "And that was right after you and I had spoken. Those things added up to suspicious behavior."

Callie narrowed her eyes. "Only if you have a suspicious mind. But I have to admit, I was suspicious about you, too." She exhaled and parked her own hands on her curvy hips, mirroring his position. "So how do we shut them down?"

"What's your role at Infinite Security?" Lance asked instead of answering.

"Analyst, computer tech, generalized support. I'm trained in self-defense, MMA, and small arms," Callie said.

"My old friend Jace is with your organization. I know it has a good reputation, and it's well-run. If you're game, I have an idea ..."

"An idea that better somehow involve me and whatever's going on here."

Someone else's voice interrupted them. "D. K.? Visitors are on the way back here, so if you're looking for privacy, man, you better find somewhere else."

The advice came from a crew member assigned to prep the area for the Living Chess Game. He was a thin young man in peasant's clothes, with a bright yellow armband tight around his left bicep, identifying him as staff.

"Thanks, Kevin. I've got to get to the other side of the fairgrounds, anyway." Lance grabbed Callie's hand to pull her along with him.

"Are you often 'looking for privacy' with female festival visitors?" Callie asked.

He couldn't quite identify the inflection in her tone, but there definitely was one. Lance decided to answer her direct question with a direct answer. "I never look for privacy with anyone here, unless it has to do with my investigation."

He took her down a narrow path that headed away from the wide one they'd used to access the Chess field. The smaller path was marked with another wooden sign declaring "Staff Only." The path curved sharply to the left. Almost immediately, they passed several people in elaborate costumes, followed by others in peasant clothing who were hauling wooden wagons filled with supplies.

Lance exchanged one-word greetings with a few of them, but didn't slow his pace. He tightened his hold on Callie's fingers, glad she hadn't pulled her hand away. Her hand felt good in his, but he wasn't going to wonder why. He wasn't going to think about that at all, because it was irrelevant. Her gentle fragrance of wildflowers and something else he couldn't identify made Lance think of sunshine days by the ocean... a fanciful thought, which was surprising, because he wasn't prone to fanciful thinking.

A thin woman outfitted in head-to-toe medieval garb hurried past them on the pathway. Working almost every day in this fanciful setting was definitely influencing his mind.

Around another sharp turn in the heavily tree-lined path, several large tents came into view. One of them had side panels in place. The trees around them absorbed some of the sound, but the constant hum of conversation punctuated by occasional laughter still filled the air.

Lance answered Callie's unspoken question. "Costume department, staff supplies, medical for regular staff and performers," Lance said by way of explanation. "The core of the behind the scenes workings."

"It's a huge set-up."

"This festival is big enough to warrant it." Lance finally released her hand and pointed at a narrower path that seemed to wind around the tents. "We can go this way and have some privacy to talk on the way back to the main fairgrounds."

Callie fell into step beside him again.

As they moved away from the noise of the staging tents, Lance explained a little more. "The first thing is for you to get authorization from your bosses to assist on this." He kept up his pace but looked over at her again. "I don't want to stir up a hornet's nest with your company."

"Don't you need the same?" Callie pointed out, "You don't know all that much about me. You're just going to trust me?"

"I explained how much I really do know already. And as I've already demonstrated by sharing info with you, I know enough to believe you can provide some backup support here. I'm authorized to make that call given the exigent circumstances." He didn't see any point in telling her that he'd already run it by his own boss, even though he didn't technically have to do that. "I think you could possibly gather additional useful information. No one here is familiar with you yet."

"What kind of information?"

"Anyone you observe acting oddly or suspiciously, particularly in the merchant areas. You'll have to behave like any other ordinary visitor. Get to know the place a little more, keep your eyes open."

"If I see something, how do I contact you here?"

"I have a cell phone on me at all times, but I have to keep it out of sight whenever possible. It's an anachronistic item, and the head of the festival is a stickler about that."

"I can imagine. No one wants to see a medieval knight on smart phone."

Lance pulled his phone out of an inside pocket in his tunic. "Your number?"

Callie rattled it off, and he immediately sent her a text.

"Now you have my number." Lance stopped walking and faced her on the path. "I'm taking a big chance here, on you, but this is important. I just want your eyes and ears involved. No matter what you see, or don't see, hear, suspect, or anything else, you only observe. I can't explain everything to you now, but this is dangerous, Callie."

Her serious expression matched his. "I get that. I'm used to it."

"Good. Unless you see or hear something you urgently need to tell me, this is it for our contact today. When you leave, get that authorization from Infinite if you can. Then I can give you more details tonight."

"Where do you want to meet?"

"Your cabin at the B&B. 8 o'clock work for you?"

"Do I even want to know how you know where I'm staying?"

"It wasn't hard to figure out. Even when you're on vacation, a beautiful woman like you should be more careful." Lance gave her one of the shallow bows he utilized at the festival. "Until we meet again."

Chapter 12

Callie

At precisely 8 o'clock that evening, Callie sat across from Lance in the small seating area of her cabin behind the B&B. Dax Mead, the founder of Infinite Security, and Rick Anderson, head of the tech department (and her direct), both agreed she could provide support to Lance McDermott.

Rick had teased her though, "Support, Callie. Don't take over his whole investigation." Could she help it if she had good ideas and wasn't shy about expressing that? She knew Rick was teasing, and her input was valued, but the experience had shown her that often wasn't the case.

The cozy cabin seemed twice as small with Lance inside it. He was tall, muscular but lean, with wide shoulders and big presence that commanded attention. She worked with men who were physically bigger, but none who she found quite so overwhelming. It was something she recognized in the open fairgrounds of the Renaissance Festival, but now in the bungalow it was exceedingly distracting.

Lance accepted the glass of iced tea she offered him, which was provided in the kitchenette fridge courtesy of the B&B. There was a small stack of wooden coasters in a decorative holder on the coffee table. Callie noted how he put one on the side table next to him before he set down his glass. It was a seemingly insignificant thing, but she thought it told her a little something about who he was as a person.

She wasn't sure what, but it told her something.

Pleasantries exchanged, she brought up the first topics she wanted to address. "Infinite is on board with me providing support for your op, given what we currently know. I need to be able to rely on your transparency with this. So, does your team have a theory about this antiquities ring you're chasing? How could these people be making enough money on the items they are dealing in to make it worth their while?"

"I'll be as transparent with you as possible, whenever possible. I can promise that, but some things will be confidential and not share-able. I don't anticipate any of those things impacting what we do here." Lance slowly tapped a long index finger against the swirl of wood at the end of the chair's arm rest. "I prefer to not share theories quite yet, and instead get your opinions without undue influence."

"What makes you think I'll have my own opinions about it?"

At that, one corner of his mouth tipped up and what was decidedly a smirk. "From what I understand, you are good at developing theories and opinions, and you aren't afraid to share them."

"Is that a problem for you?" Callie challenged.

"Not at all. As I said, I'll welcome any considered opinions you come up with."

He was being surprisingly reasonable. Although maybe that wasn't a fair assessment. Why did she think he'd be *unreasonable*? Because he's a grumbly alpha male? Or again, is that just his "character"? He'd been nice at dinner, but then again, he had also been collecting information about her the whole time, hadn't he?

Unaware of the debate going on in Callie's mind, Lance continued addressing the initial questions. "Individual items could go for anywhere from a couple hundred thousand to several million dollars," he said. "It all adds up."

Callie forced her attention to remain solely on his words; she'd analyze is personality and motives after he left. "I get that. But isn't time of the essence somehow? If it wasn't, you could simply wait for new backup from your own organization. This isn't a social experiment, or a test case." She leaned back and crossed her own legs. "Refusing to share your theories is wasting time. What's you and your team's best guess on this? Are these people just exploiting a revenue stream? Funding weapons acquisitions? Supplementing drug money?"

He leaned forward and braced his elbows just above his knees.

She could see that he was deciding what to tell her, and it ticked her off enough that she wasn't going to be silent about it. "If you want me involved on the frontline in this, then you treat me as a partner and a teammate. Otherwise, I'm already out and you can leave."

"No need to be offended, Callie. You realize this is highly sensitive info."

"If you know as much about me as you claim to, then you know I have high security clearances, and plenty of experience dealing with highly sensitive info." Callie stood up from her chair. "I think you better keep this mission within your own people. I'm not getting involved in something where I have to rely on your judgment about what I need to know." She knew she sounded derisive but couldn't bring herself to care. "I know what my team told me about you, but outside of that, all I know is that you like to play dress-up and scowl at people. Not my scene."

She walked around the chair and over to the door. Either she was in, or she was out, she wasn't settling for being halfway involved. Any job involving any fieldwork was potentially dangerous. No way was she participating with limited information, partial understanding, and zero familiarity with those involved. Putting that level of trust in strangers would be the height of stupidity and foolishness.

It didn't matter that her boss, Dax, had approved "lending" her to Lance and his team. That he'd agreed they were trustworthy and legit, and even said he knew some of the people at the company. It was ultimately *her* decision to make, and she had her own standards to uphold.

"Good luck to you," Callie said as she opened the door for him to leave.

Lance hadn't moved, except to once again sit back in the armchair. While they'd been talking, the sun had set, and the lamps in the seating area cast shadows as much as they did light. The dramatic lighting painted his face in shadows and obscured the color of his eyes. Still, she could see that they were steadily fixed upon her, and she remembered how steely gray they'd been outside at the festival.

He spoke quietly, evidently unperturbed by her words or gesture of dismissal. "Callie, I can't speak more about any of this with the door wide open."

She stood there unmoving for another full minute, then pushed the door closed and locked it. Instead of returning to her seat, Callie leaned back against the heavy wood with her arms crossed. Her own gaze remained firmly fixed on him, And she resolved to ignore the potent magnetism of his presence in the confined space, no matter how difficult that was proving to be.

"Speak, then," she said.

Chapter 13

Callie

"There's been more than one link found to a mid-level operative in a terrorist cell Homeland has had an eye on for a while. A disillusioned American, in his mid-20s."

She hadn't expected to hear *that*. Callie moved away from the door and again stood behind the chair facing his. "If there's a terrorist link at all, why isn't Homeland all over it? Or one of the other alphabet agencies?"

"World politics. Cultural sensitivity. Strained resources. Lack of corroboration." Lance shook his head, the slight twist to his lips the only indication that he was disgusted by the inaction. "All of the above or something else."

"You think the American 20-something came up with this on his own?" Callie asked skeptically. "What kind of background and connections does he have? Do you know his name?"

"Doubtful he developed this alone. Regardless, he's making a name for himself with his superiors by bringing substantial money into the fold." Lance crossed one long leg over the other. "The name he writes on receipts is Tom Cooper."

When Lance rested his right ankle on the opposing knee, Callie got a glimpse of dark socks with silver shields on them. She didn't say anything, just let her eyes linger there. He laughed. "From the Festival, as if you couldn't guess."

"They probably sell a lot of those," she commented. "A lot more than replica weapons." Callie shifted her commentary back to the other piece of information Lance had just shared. "Tom Cooper is about as wholesome and uninteresting a name as you could get. 99.9% sure it's a fake."

"Agreed," he said. "Both his name and his appearance allow him to blend into the crowd."

That comment was also startling. "Have you or one of your colleagues actually seen the guy? In person or on security tapes?"

"We found out after the fact that two of us did, including me. Damn if I could remember him after the fact! I had been present when he was completing a purchase, and I couldn't recall anything about him at all." Lance didn't bother trying to disguise his disgust at his failure to notice the transaction that happened near him.

"Security footage didn't help?"

"No. He had on nondescript clothing, and a dark blue baseball cap pulled down low that totally shadowed his face. He knew where the cameras were and never looked toward any of them." Lance shoved a hand through his dark hair, leaving it in surprisingly stylish disarray.

Obviously, the suspect was clever.

"Not even on others after he walked away from the merchant?" Callie asked.

"There aren't all that many cameras on the grounds of the Festival. They are primarily at the entrance gates, around the merchants, and where they sell alcohol. There are some wide-angle ones covering an assortment of large areas, like the jousting field. But that's it."

Callie moved around the chair and dropped into it again. "I need to see that video. I understand his face isn't visible, but I need to see what I can see. The way he stands, moves, gestures, how he's built. Anything I can."

He laced his fingers behind his neck and stretched his back. "Sorry, the armor leaves your upper back stiff. I'll show you the video, but it has to be on my computer."

"Absolutely, I understand." She couldn't blame him for wanting to take that type of precaution. After all, she'd do exactly the same thing if their roles were reversed. Callie pulled her mobile phone out of a zippered pocket in her shorts and gestured toward him with it. "I want to take notes. This device and its connection is highly secured, totally encrypted."

"I'm sure it is."

She unlocked the phone with the necessary series of codes, then resumed the conversation exactly where she'd interrupted it a minute earlier.

"Explain to me again how you figured this out?" Callie's fingers flew across the screen as she configured a document in her modified Notes app.

Lance watched her closely, but didn't comment on what she was doing. He simply answered her question: "I'll get to that. About your other question, even if the merchant ever had access to an authentic piece such as the one sold in the transaction, there was no way he had it just laying around for a mistake to be made."

Callie nibbled at the left side of her bottom lip as she thought about it. It didn't make sense at all. "Investigating that merchant didn't lead anywhere?"

"No. The merchant's name is Robert McKendrick. He was totally cooperative, has been in business for decades, and from what we could learn, he appears completely reputable. He turned over his records without hesitation and agreed to keep this quiet while we figure it out. Even his own people have no idea about this. He wants us to put a stop to it before word gets out and reflects badly on him and his company."

"Company name?"

"Modern Medieval, Inc."

Callie added that info to the notes she was making. "Then the switch was made at the Festival itself, or on the way to it," Callie mused. Another question occurred to her. "Is it common that the merchant has a name on an item that's waiting for someone to pick it up? Do people actually buy a ticket to the event just to pick up something they ordered in advance?"

"We were told that yes, it happens frequently enough to be considered a regular thing. Observation on site bears that out." He elaborated, "Modern Medieval has a website, online and paper catalog, and does what they call targeted mailings. They also advertise in industry publications and newsletters."

Callie was startled by that information. "There are Renaissance industry things that they advertise in? I've never seen anything like that."

"Yes, it was news to me, too. It's a hobby like with Cosplay or Civil War reenactors. Some people are casually interested, and others are borderline obsessed, and everything in between. Taken altogether, there's a sizable audience or market for Renaissance replica clothing, merchandise, and festivals."

Callie's analytical thinking was in overdrive. "Would Cooper's bosses be all that interested in something so small scale as his set-up? I mean, it seems like it's very luck of the draw, isn't it?"

Lance looked at her quizzically. "Meaning what exactly?"

"I'm thinking a lot of things simultaneously, so I'll try to break them down." Callie took another moment to marshal her thoughts. "If someone is passing along real antiquities, someone working in league with Cooper, do they know exactly what they're getting in each transaction?"

"What's the alternative? That it's the luck of the draw?" He appeared to think about it but then shook his head. "That doesn't make sense, because they have to be prepared to pay, and how would they know how much money to have on hand?"

"Bear with me. Related to that, where is the supplier getting these authentic items from? It's not like there can be an endless supply, right?" She tipped her head back against the seat and closed her eyes, thinking the puzzle through. "And then Cooper, his terrorist colleagues, or their agents, need to find a buyer for every item. Every time they have to find a buyer is more potential exposure for them. And if they don't have a buyer lined up already, they have to store the antiquity or whatever until they do find a buyer."

Callie opened her eyes and scowled at him. "One of the big problems here is that you still haven't told me how you and your company became aware of all this in the first place."

"To answer your question about Cooper and whoever he's working with finding buyers, it's likely they're using an intermediary of some kind, precisely for that reason," Lance agreed. "I became involved with this when the company took this job as a favor to a client who had suspicions that the replica sword his wife bought at a Renaissance Festival on its the closing day in Florida was, in fact, the real thing, and not a replica at all."

"And it turned out he was right."

"Yes. The festival in Florida closed the last week of June. The one here opened a couple of weeks later."

Callie was finding the whole thing interesting, even outside the case at hand. "Same vendors?"

"Most of them. Every location includes local artisans and craftspeople, but many of the niche merchants stay the same, or at least make frequent appearances." Lance shifted and put his foot on the floor again. "A lot of them have popular social media accounts, with lots of followers and engagement."

"Including the one your client's wifebought the sword from?"

"Right."

Callie had an alarming thought. "Where is that sword now? If they know who they gave it to by mistake–"

"It's in a secure location," Lance assured her. "The wife made sure to tell multiple people in public places that she bought a great replica at the Festival and gifted it to a friend. She also shared that on her social media. Hopefully, that gets the spotlight off her."

"Unless they grab her to make her tell them who she gave it to," Callie pointed out.

"She has a personal protection detail assigned to her. As I mentioned before, her husband was already a Golden client."

He *had* said that, she remembered that of course, but it still wasn't a guarantee that they had thought about the wife's vulnerabilities. She started to ask another question but Lance was already shaking his head. "If you're going to ask why he's a client, I can't tell you that. Confidentiality. I can tell you it's completely unrelated to this matter, but it does involve protecting her at all times."

Callie laughed at that. "It's almost embarrassing that you already know me well enough to anticipate what I was going to say."

"Analysts need data, right?" He gave her a small half-smile. "I figured that would be the next logical next question."

She nodded, then moved on. "Backtracking, if these pieces – these antiquities – can't always be guaranteed to bring in huge amounts of money, what's the benefit of taking the risk of being caught? If the risk-benefit analysis doesn't decidedly skew in the favor of whoever's running it, why bother?"

"We think there's something bigger at play here."

"Bigger how?"

"In scale. I don't think it's just the transaction of selling the item that's bringing in money. I believe there's a bigger play with wider reach involved."

"Wider reach in terms of what?" Callie tried to follow his line of thought. "In terms of where the money is being funneled? In terms of what they're going to do with it?"

"It goes back to what you mentioned earlier. If we are right about Tom Cooper, and he's raising money to support the Taliban or one of its splinter groups, then it's got to be a bigger operation to get their attention. Profiling says that recognition and attention is just as important to someone like Cooper as any allegiance he might have to their cause, or beliefs, or goals."

"Recognition and attention for bigger amounts of money and bigger levels of destruction," Callie mused.

"You wanted to know our theory. That's the overarching one."

"I get that. But how does the bigger operation come into it? And what's the bigger operation?"

"We've looked into other niche hobbies and interests, like we talked about—"

"Like Cosplay?"

"Right. We didn't come up with anything, although we are still keeping an ear to the ground on those things. Just in case."

Callie shook her head. "If you're right and this guy Cooper is the one running his antiquities game successfully, it seems unlikely he would dilute his efforts and his time. I mean, why risk taking his eyes away from what's working for him?" She paused. "Also, what makes you think the guy you saw wasn't just there for the pickup, or a courier? Would the person running the operation really want to risk himself by being at the center of the transaction?"

"I agree, but the information Eckert received a couple of times from an anonymous source indicated Cooper has a controlling personality and doesn't trust people."

"From a good source?" Callie raised her eyebrows at him when she asked the question. Sources and tips could be invaluable during any investigation, but they could also be manipulated, disinformation, red herrings, and a distraction from other solid Intel.

"All I can tell you about that is yes, he or she has been a good source."

Chapter 14

Callie

Just like on her previous visits to the Renaissance Festival, Callie parked her car in the public lots and took the shuttle bus to the main entrance gate. She waited in line and when it was her turn, used cash to pay for a two-day ticket this time. Purchasing a longer multi-day admission ticket might attract attention, and she didn't want to do that. If she had any hope of seeing, overhearing, or stumbling into some useful information, she had to be just another typical visitor to the fairgrounds.

On her way through the gates, Callie kept close to a group of fellow festival goers who were chattering amongst themselves and taking in the sights around them. She likewise took everything in, although she was looking for Lance, not just whoever and whatever caught her eye.

As the group began to break up and its members moved off in multiple directions, Callie headed for the merchant area. She made a conscious effort to blend in with the shoppers already crowding the busy area. Callie kept her baseball cap low over her face, and her eyes focused on things directly in front of her and below her primary line of sight. She didn't do anything that would potentially draw attention to her; no big movements, no overly enthusiastic gestures, nothing that would stand out among the crowd.

Callie wandered from one merchant to another, doing her best to appear like her shopping pattern was random, although in truth her approach was deliberate and intended to make certain she didn't miss anything. At each merchant, she took her time and thoroughly studied the wares being offered for sale. One merchant sold floral headpieces crafted of artificial flowers, another had jewelry on offer. There were decorative pieces for the home, a booth with heraldry and coats of arms, another with dishware and recipe books. Multiple merchants had goods that were purely modern mixed with pieces inspired by medieval times.

There were several dealers in medieval armor and weaponry of many types, ranging from small pieces to large shields and long spears. Swords and other potentially dangerous items were displayed on boards and racks higher than the reach of the crow. Small, lacquered signs advising interested persons to "Ask for Assistance."

Callie looked at her watch more than once. The first time, she'd been at the Renaissance Festival for more than an hour. When she next checked, she'd been there two and a half hours. Three hours. Her enthusiasm for shopping waned well before the two-hour mark.

It wasn't the first time she been tasked with a live surveillance or reconnaissance assignment. She was uneasy, more than she'd expected to be. Yes, she wasn't quite as comfortable with a different agency behind her, and that was undoubtedly part of it. There was more, though. Something like the feeling she had when she'd first seen Lance – a suspicious, swirling feeling in her stomach that set off internal alarm bells. Only this time, instead of generating something akin to excitement, the feeling was foreboding more than anything else.

Callie picked up a 10-inch tall sculpture of a knight on horse-back, the man's armor painted in shades of blue. She turned it over in her hands, her head bent towards it and her eyes still roving around the area as best she could. *Where is Lance?* It was too early for the daily exhibition on the jousting field, and therefore much too early for the actual jousting competition. She replaced the brightly painted knight onto the shelf and moved further down the row.

"If you like that, have you seen these?" The speaker was a tall, blonde woman wearing a navy-blue baseball cap similar to the one on Callie's own head. "I doubt they had goblets like these in medieval times, but who knows, right?"

She held a pair of pewter -colored goblets in her hands, each one decorated with an image of a knight on horseback, one wearing red and the other wearing blue. Callie looked from the items to the woman's face.

Her own small laugh was sincere. "I think that's a pretty solid guess." She tried to take in as much about the other woman's appearance as possible without making her interest obvious. "Although since women tied good luck tokens on the lances, there must have been fan girls even if there wasn't merchandising."

The woman replaced the goblets on the shelf from which she'd removed them. "Is this your first time at the festival?"

"No," Callie said. "You?"

"No." The stranger's gaze was surprisingly cold, despite her earlier friendly words. "The attractions at these festivals can be surprisingly dangerous. Be careful."

Before Callie could process the strange morning and form a reply, the woman turned and left the merchant's tent through the closest opening. Callie felt compelled to immediately follow, although she didn't see the woman when she got to the partitioned doorway. There were people milling about, and others walking in every direction, and Callie had no way to know which way the woman she sought had gone.

Callie browsed the merchant's wares for a bit longer, and then she moved on to the next one. That tent held real and artificial crowns, circlets, and clips of wearable flowers, along with wreaths and posies that could be displayed in the home. The luscious fragrance of assorted flowers perfumed the air inside it, adding to the feeling of having stumbled into a greenhouse of sorts. Callie wanted to purchase something from amongst the beautiful offerings, but didn't want to risk carrying packages that might slow her down or hinder her movements. Sure, she was supposed to be simply on the lookout for suspicious people or behaviors, but she needed to be prepared for anything. Even the simplest situations could go awry.

Drawing attention to herself while she wandered through the rest of the festival was another concern – although her encounter told her that she was already the subject of someone's attention. The feeling left her uneasy and uncomfortable, but it wasn't entirely unwanted. After all, the goal was to see who or what looked in any way suspicious. If she'd somehow drawn out a party of interest, all she had to do was identify him, her, them.

At least another hour passed by the time Callie exited the booth of the last merchant in the row. A wide footpath cut through the merchant area, and she took a moment to decide if she should visit the booths on that side of the path or go deeper into the overall section and then circle back. Although she wasn't searching for anyone or anything in particular, she wanted to follow a grid search pattern, for the sake of efficiency.

She and Lance weren't supposed to seek each other out, but if she encountered him organically, by chance, she was going to let him know her suspicions. And she was definitely going to mention the blonde woman who'd spoken to her in what she perceived as odd way. Could she be the same woman Crowley had mentioned when she spotted the man with Lance?

Chapter 15

The next day ...

Callie

After a second day of hanging around the Renaissance Festival carrying out her surveillance assignment – a day that passed almost identically to the first – Callie paced around her bungalow. She spoke to Lance on a secure line, repeating what she'd already told him. It was a challenge, but she kept her voice level. Nice and calm.

"Like yesterday, nothing really stood out to me at all today. The only exception was that small interaction with the blonde woman yesterday, which I told you about yesterday. Even that wasn't particularly telling or anything; it was just a little weird."

"Did you see her again today?"

"No."

"No other people caught your eye?" Lance pressed. "Were there any strange things? Things that stood out?"

"Lance, almost in everybody is in costume, or they rigged up their own version of one. Or they are wearing tourist clothes."

"Good point," he admitted. "But you know what I mean."

"The odds of this approach being productive are really slim. I know you must know that." He had to realize it was the equivalent of looking for a needle in a haystack. "I should be spending my time around the businesses where these suspect transactions would be taking place."

Lance replied so quickly that their words all but collided. "You can't spend ten hours a day hovering around Modern Medieval. It'll be too noticeable and that will probably either scare them off or cause some unpredictable reaction."

"I get that. But still—"

Lance completely interrupted her that time. "There are other businesses that could potentially be used for illicit antiquities dealings. You should also keep an eye on those."

"Yes, I identified a couple that have merchandise to potentially fit the brief." Callie envisioned two retailers who had items that weren't weaponry but mimicked other authentic antiquities. "Both of the other shops are somewhat smaller and because they're in tent structures, shoppers stand out more. You don't think so?"

He had to agree with her about that because it was so obvious. "They are good-sized but are in enclosed spaces with aisles set up to prevent shoplifting. If I linger, it's going to be obvious."

"Make actionable suggestions, and I'll consider them." Callie could picture the determined set of Lance's job as he said that. "I'm certainly willing to listen to anything you have to say."

If only that was true... she'd also be saying a whole lot about how good he looked when he was intense and serious, how great he smelled when he stood close to her, how warm and smooth his biceps were when she grabbed onto him the other day. And how often she found herself wondering how he'd taste if she convinced herself to be brave enough to find out.

* * *

Lance

He told her, "I'm certainly willing to listen to anything you have to say."

There was a long silence. In his mind's eye, Lance pictured Callie closing her eyes for an extended time the way he noticed she did when she was focusing on a burgeoning thought. What was he going to say?

Did she have a brainstorm about effectively surveilling the critical parts of the Renaissance Festival? Would she think of something that he hadn't? There hadn't been time to fill her in on every last detail of his investigation, but fresh eyes on a problem often noticed something the original team did not.

Or will she surprise him? Tell him she had as many unprofessional thoughts about him as he had about her? Invite him over to her cabin at the B&B so they could spend some time discussing the case. Naked, in her bed. Or on the couch. Or on the floor. Hell, he'd be happy to work with anything and everything she might suggest.

Callie finally said, "I'll think it all through again tonight."

She sounded tired. Lance put his phone on speaker and set it down on the dresser in his motel room. He ran both hands roughly through his hair. "Thanks, Callie. You're supposed to be on vacation, relaxing, and I dragged you into *this*."

Lance heard the smile hidden in Callie's voice when she said, "As I remember it, I enthusiastically volunteered. But you're welcome."

* * *

And the day after that...
Callie

Callie sat in an Adirondack-style chair on the front porch of her small bungalow. She stretched her legs out in front of her and flexed her ankles. Standing around all day in the heat and accomplishing nothing had her on edge. And it was surprisingly uncomfortable.

As was watching Lance talk to too many women.

Yes, it was part of his job. And yes, he stayed in character for the most part, being aloof, mysterious, and growly. Lance, as the Dark Knight, embodied the medieval bad boy and apparently had universal appeal. In Callie's experience so far, real-life Lance was just as growly– even if he wasn't quite as aloof and mysterious to her anymore.

Callie knew all that was irrelevant. She was well aware that her role in his investigation came about purely by chance. It was convenient for Lance to have somebody to fill a short-term staffing gap, and for her to distract from the tedium of an unwanted "vacation".

They were temporary colleagues and nothing more.

Every time she spoke to Lance, her visceral reaction to him surprised her. When it was on the phone, just the sound of his voice, without his overwhelming physical presence, electrified her senses. Callie forced herself to focus on the reason for her call.

"Still another day done, and I discovered nothing. Unless you're interested in knowing how many times the garbage gets emptied near Modern Medieval, or what the most popular snack foods are in that area at different times of the day."

"Most days, garbage is emptied every two hours." Lance responded without commenting on the sarcasm she hadn't bothered hiding. "The most popular snack throughout the entire day is popcorn. Breaking it down more precisely, mini muffins are the most popular in the morning, and sausages on sticks later in the day, but *overall,* it's popcorn."

She heard him moving around. There was an increase in the noise on his end of the call and she tried to identify the sounds.

He spoke again. "If you want more specificity or info about beverage sales, let me know."

"Seriously?" Callie was incredulous. "You know all that how? An inside track with sanitation? Covertly accessing vendor receipts?" The noise behind Lance quieted down. "Where are you?"

"I've got to go," he said abruptly.

Before she could reply, the dial tone was all that remained on the line with her. "You do that."

Callie jabbed the red dot on her own phone to disconnect her side of the call. Silently she missed the old landline phone in her grandmother's house. Slamming down the receiver was much more satisfying than digitally disconnecting.

* * *

Lance

Enough was enough already.

He'd been buried in this investigation for months. Going through evidence, exploring ideas with his team, participating in research, formulating more theories and possibilities. Gaining detailed understanding about the Renaissance fair and festival circuit. Polishing and expanding upon the horseback riding skills he'd acquired when he was a kid and a teenager visiting Uncle Gordon's Wyoming ranch for summer vacations and every other chance he could get.

Bonfire and tailgate nights there were cherished memories that could never be re-created. Nights of tired camaraderie and others of tense survival during his military years were equally valuable in their own way. His work in private security recaptured some of that. *Sometimes.*

Tonight, he'd spent several hours hunkered down in his car while hiding in plain sight in the parking lot of the one big box stores in the area. They unearthed a tip that items of interest were handed off sometimes in this lot, and something would be going down at a particular time tonight. Lance arrived more than an hour early and stayed two hours past the time he was given but had seen nothing. All he saw were harried people trying to squeeze in their errands at the end of a long day.

Some things he couldn't make happen just because he wanted to.

And some, he could.

Chapter 16

Callie

Fifteen minutes later, showered and wearing the plush B&B provided bathrobe again, Callie checked her phone for the third time. She still had service – a full five bars. Lance hadn't called and hadn't texted. Unless a bathroom emergency had been calling his name, that was just plain rude. If he'd gotten another call he needed to take, he could have said something and not just vanished from the line, leaving her to wonder and worry.

So rude.

Callie glared at her phone once more for good measure then stomped over to the small refrigerator. No, she corrected her, she didn't stomp, she walked purposefully. That was a better description. She wasn't a petulant toddler having a tantrum; she was smart, capable, and professional.

Callie opened the freezer with a sharp tug.

She was deciding between the three frozen meals she'd stocked the freezer with the previous day. It didn't make sense to keep shelling out money for lunch and dinner every day when there was a perfectly good microwave in her cabin. The faux leather folio in the bungalow listed places visitors could buy groceries – a local small supermarket, a farmer's market, a gas station with an attachment minimart, and a big box store a bit further away. Callie had stopped into the local supermarket and purchased some easy meals. She had a frozen Three Cheese Rigatoni in one hand and Flatbread Margarita Pizza in the other when someone knocked on the cabin door.

"Seriously?" she muttered. Callie shoved both boxes back into the freezer and shoved her irritation aside. Every evening, a staff member from the B&B brought to each bungalow some fresh-baked cookies, fresh fruit, or other little treat. It was a nice touch.

Tonight, she was irritable though.

After tightening the tie on her bathrobe, Callie opened the door with a friendly greeting on her lips – one that immediately vanished. "What are you doing here?"

Lance had the audacity to smirk at her. "Nice greeting."

"I'm surprised to see you." She stepped back to allow him to enter. "Why didn't you say you were coming here?"

The cooler night air clung to him when he moved into her space. "It was a last-minute decision."

"After we got off the phone?" Callie held up a finger to signal that he should wait before he spoke. "After *you* got off the phone, that is. You didn't have the courtesy to ask if there was anything else I wanted to say before you hung up on me." She pressed her lips together tightly. "So then, I was concerned that something was happening to you."

"Is there something you want to say?" Lance unzipped his jacket and shrugged it off. The heather blue Henley he wore underneath was fitted close to the body, enough to subtly highlight the rounded muscles of his shoulders and the swells of his upper arms.

Callie's first instinct had been to tell him to put his jacket back on and get out, but she didn't. She didn't want him to leave. Her internal acknowledgment of that fact thoroughly distracted her from their conversation. "What?"

Lance crossed his arms and eyed her with something that looked an awful lot like amusement. "Was there anything else you wanted to say?"

"There was in that moment, yes." Callie tossed her hands up in frustration. "But now, off the top of my head, I can't recall exactly what it was." She pointed an accusatory finger at him. "And don't you tell me if it was that important, I'll remember."

"Okay." He raised his hand a little in mock surrender. "I'm sure you'll let me know." Lance's expression shifted to a more serious one. "I didn't mean to worry you, so I'm sorry for that."

Callie wanted to invite him to sit down. To offer him a drink, or a meal, or a snack. Or herself. But she wasn't going to do any of those things. He was keeping it professional and so would she. "Is something new going on with the investigation?"

"No," Lance said, taking a step toward her. "Although actually, I take that back. There is something new going on with the investigation. It's excellent, but it's also dangerous."

Callie frowned up at him. "What happened?"

"You." He reached out and put his right hand on her waist, curving it around to pull her closer. "I think about you too often, Callie. When I am at the festival, jousting, driving, doing surveillance, analyzing information, taking a shower."

Callie pressed into him, absorbing the heat of his body and his gaze.

He gently stroked her cheek with his other hand. "I want to kiss you now, not quickly like the other day, but the way I really want to. Any objections?"

Her voice came out as a whisper, but it was clear and steady. "I want that, too."

Callie didn't wait for him to kiss her; she pushed up onto her toes and slid an arm around his neck, anchoring herself to him and kissing him first. Lance accepted the invitation, his lips cool and smooth under hers. One, two, three heartbeats passed then he took over.

She felt his fingers in her hair, then cupping the back of her head, changing the angle of their connection so he could take the kiss deeper, wetter, hotter. Callie played with the hair at the back of his neck, the soft strands a tactile counterpoint to the hard muscles her other hand skated over beneath his shirt.

"Bedroom," she said.

The bungalow was small, and Lance could have easily found it on his own, but this was her decision, and she was going to own it. Callie slid her hand down to his and grasped his fingers, then led him the short distance to her bedroom.

He kicked the door shut with his foot, and it closed with a satisfying snap. That was followed by a pair of thuds as he yanked off one boot and then the other and discarded both by the door.

Callie watched him with unabashed anticipation when he pulled his Henley off over his head. She gestured at her own attire, the bathrobe soft and comfortable but not alluring.

"Now we're getting closer to an equal number of garments." She twirled the ends of the wrap tie that secured it. "Sorry this isn't sexy, but I wasn't expecting company tonight."

"That's sexy as fuck on you," he said. He ran a hand over his own jaw, his eyes burning with him as they scanned her again from head to toe and back again. "You're like a delicious gift I can't wait to unwrap."

Lance closed the small distance between them and then his mouth was on hers again and time ceased to exist as he licked and nipped at her lips, his tongue tasting and tangling with hers.

Callie swallowed his low moan and fed him one of her own. She pulled back slightly to survey his sculpted chest and well-defined abdominal wall. Her fingertips followed the path of her eyes and traced random patterns through the smattering of hair that highlighted his musculature.

Lance moved his hands to the fabric holding her robe together. Holding her gaze with his own, he made quick work of untying it and pulling the strip of fabric away. With his fingertips, he traced her collarbones that continued on toward her shoulders. Lance used his knuckles to nudge the lapels to the sides until the robe dropped to the floor with a whoosh.

Without the robe, the air felt cool, and Callie shivered in reaction. Her nipples tightened into hard peaks from both the cold air and the heat of Lance's perusal.

"Incredible," he murmured before he leaned forward, and his mouth got busy doing other things. He cupped one breast in his slightly callused hand and licked then suckled the other. He switched back and forth until her knees were weak.

Callie clutched at his bicep with one hand, the other latching onto his belt loop. "Lance!"

"I've got you, sweetheart." Lance guided her the few steps to the bed. The B&B hadn't scrimped on the quality of its mattresses or bedding, and although she appreciated it each night when she went to sleep, she was grateful for it even more at the moment.

Callie worked on opening Lance's jeans. She'd been enjoying the feel of his arousal through the denim, but she wanted to get his length in her hand. In her mouth. She needed to get closer now, to feel the heat of his skin without fabric between them.

"Slow down, Callie," Lance cautioned. "I don't want to short-circuit this, and I want you too much to let you touch me right now."

"I don't know what to say to that." She really didn't. Could he possibly be that worked up from kissing her and the limited touching they'd done thus far?

Lance laughed, softly, tracing his fingers lightly up and down her thighs. "Don't you understand how incredible you are?"

Callie's breath hitched when he lowered his head to kiss the other side of her breast again. He kissed higher up on her breast and her chest rose to meet him, anticipation firing her blood. His touch moved to the apex of her thighs, tracing then exploring her there. Callie was embarrassed by her own slickness, but Lance made appreciative sounds. Hungry sounds.

Callie again tried to open the fastening of his jeans, and this time Lance helped. While he used her wetness to stroke and circle the bundle of nerves that incited so much pleasure for her, she slipped her hand inside his briefs. She'd felt the general size and shape of him through his jeans, but the velvety hardness and heat of him made her heart beat faster in anticipation.

The sounds of rising passions were no match for the strident sound of a phone ringing.

"Ignore it." Lance teased her entrance with one thick finger, then resumed the tracing motion with which he'd been tormenting her. "You feel so good, Callie."

Callie wanted to say so much – "you feel so big", "so hard", "so hot", "best kisses ever", "keep touching me." All those words and more hovered on her lips but she couldn't manage to say them, just lost herself in the moments and the magic of his touch as he coaxed her higher and higher toward the pinnacle of her release.

His short touch and his continued whispers of encouragement extended those climactic moments until the ringing of her phone came again. "Do you have to get that?" she asked. "It's the second time it's ringing."

Lance snickered softly against her neck. "It's the fourth time, actually, I think you were distracted for the last two and missed them." He dropped a kiss on her lips and reluctantly pulled away from her to grab the phone from where he'd left it on the top of the dresser.

He looked at the display and his expression quickly morphed from aroused to tense. Lance seemed to receive a message he didn't like. His rueful expression said it before his words did. "I have to leave, Callie. I'm sorry."

Lying naked on the bed, Callie awkwardly watched him adjust himself and his briefs and wrestle his jeans closed. As he jammed his feet into his boots, she clutched the pillow to her front and tried to reach where her robe lay on the floor. His attire already in place, Lance held up the robe for her to slip into. She felt ridiculous as she stood clutching the pillow and turned to slide her arms into the sleeves. He lifted her hair out from the collar and let it fall down the back of the garment.

Instead of clutching the pillow she switched to clutching the sides of the robe together and faced him. Lance had the bathrobe belt in hand, and he carefully positioned it around her waist.

Callie cleared her throat. "I'm the one who's sorry. I mean, you didn't get to... I mean, you're not..." And again, she knew she was blushing like some shy, inexperienced mess.

Lance it drew her into the circle of his arms and held her for a minute. "I'm a grown man, Callie. It's okay."

Callie nodded, unsure what else to say.

"Walk me out? Make sure you lock the door behind me."

Callie followed him into the short hallway and across the room to the front door. It was on the tip of her tongue to say something snarky about how she didn't need to be reminded to lock up, but she didn't.

Lance grabbed his jacket before he walked out the door. "Lock up," he said again. "Good night."

"Good night," Callie echoed.

Then he was gone.

Chapter 17

Lance

Two days after their kisses and exploration in Callie's bungalow, the physical tension between them was better, and at the same time, much worse. He should have known better than to touch her that way. But when she'd reciprocated so enthusiastically, well, his lifelong history of making sound decisions flew right out the window.

He'd have to unpack that another day.

Lance stared at the tree in consternation, more than a little shocked by what he was seeing. A small dagger was thrust through an unlined page that definitely resembled a scroll, both of them splattered with what looked like blood. He didn't need to remove it to read the message printed there in bold, block letters: **Partners are weaknesses..**

The meaning and the message were chilling and crystal clear. Since the message was left here, somehow his cover was apparently blown. And so, possibly, was Callie's connection to him. There was a chance that whoever left the note was referring to one of the men working with him, but he couldn't take that risk. Lance pulled his phone out of its hiding place inside his shirt and speed-dialed Drew.

His backup answered on the second ring. Lance wasted no time on pleasantries.

"They know who I am. Meeting location one is compromised." He snapped a picture of the dagger and the note. "Need to bag this and cut her loose."

There was no need to explain either of those things. Instead, Drew asked practical questions. "Do you have what you need for disposal? And do you know where she is, if they are referring to her?"

"I can manage both."

Dealing with the components of the threat was going to be much simpler than dealing with Callie.

In a hollowed-out log less than 50 feet away from the meeting point, Lance kept some basic supplies – including a couple of self-sealing plastic bags and multiple pairs of nitrile gloves. It was simple to slip on a pair, take one of the bags, and remove the items from the tree trunk. The odds were that nothing useful would be gained from either one, but they needed to check. He also needed to make sure nobody else would see them.

At least if somebody had, the person who left them had styled them in keeping with the Renaissance theme. Lance couldn't take time to thoroughly examine the "blood" on the note right now, but upon closer inspection, to his naked eye, the blood appeared more theatrical than real. He wasn't a medical professional, but he'd seen more of the real stuff than most average people would have. This blood was too scarlet, less brown, and the spatter pattern was not consistent with any realistic injury. The directional tails of the drops were mostly missing, indicating that the blood was dripped on the paper from directly overhead. There was also a sugary smell that was consistent with fake blood, but perhaps there was other trace or even partial prints that the lab could find.

After he jammed the sealed bag into his pants pocket, Lance made certain that his tunic covered any sign of the bulge from the bag. He set off in the direction of the festival's primary thoroughfare, his eyes searching for any of the suspects who'd been identified, and for Callie.

He found her watching the acrobatic performers in the massive mud pit. "Where is your car parked?"

She answered him without turning her head. "Field 2."

Lance didn't tell her details about how their quarry might know who he was and might know about her. "Go there now. Meet me in the back room at Grossman's Farm Stand on the corner of Maple and Main." Lance forced his arms over his chest, pretending great interest in the show he'd seen dozens of times. "Be extremely careful."

Callie stood in place for several more minutes, her only movement the tilting of her and head as she watched the show. After she left the scene of the performance, Lance turned away from where one of the characters was gargling a glass of muddy water and followed her at a pace that should look relaxed to a bystander.

A short while later, when Lance pulled his car into the gravel parking area in front of Grossman's, Callie's car was already there, parked at the far side. He drove around to the back of the building, where he parked his car past a couple that belonged to the business. From previous visits, he knew there was a back door, and he used it to slip into the store. The rear public entrance led him into a hallway that followed an outside wall to the midpoint of the store, and then opened into the last of three sections that made up the public part of the business.

The store wasn't busy, and he had no trouble locating Callie, who was meandering through the fresh produce displays, a shopping basket looped over her arm. Bright sunlight streamed through the windows. It illuminated her from behind and set alight the different shades of honey and gold in her hair. No matter her surroundings, she stood out. When his gaze got tangled up around her, it was about so much more than surface beauty. He wanted to learn much more about her, wanted to look deeper. Something captivating about her tugged at him deep inside in a way that was unfamiliar but not unwelcome.

Yes, his decision to cut her loose from this investigation was the right one. She wasn't going to like it, but it was the way it had to be. Lance approached her from across a display of apples, their unblemished skins shining rich, ruby red and gemstone green in the sunlight. Callie looked almost angelic in the sunlight now, but he was certain her response to being booted from his team would be anything but.

Lance did what he always did in difficult situations; he braced himself and jumped right in. No point stalling. "We need to talk." He angled his head toward the rear door. "Could you come with me, please?" His tone made it clear that the question wasn't a question at all.

Callie looked at him quizzically and gave an uncertain nod. "Sure. Do I have time to check out?"

"This can't wait."

"Oh." She looked around for a moment then put her handbasket between a display of apples and one of oranges. "I'll come back for it when we're done."

He didn't say anything to that. When they were standing next to his car, Lance glanced around again to see if anyone was nearby, then opened the passenger door. "Let's sit a minute."

Callie didn't ask any questions. When they were both inside the vehicle, she asked excitedly, "What's going on? Is there a break in the investigation? A new lead, new information?"

The vehicle wasn't even on, but Lance put his hands on the steering wheel to have something to do with them. He looked in the rearview mirror, then over at her. *No way to say it except to say it.* "You're off the team."

"Off the... What are you talking about?"

"I think my words were clear. I appreciate your efforts, but no longer require your services." Lance forced himself to make and maintain eye contact with Callie. "The situation is under control now. As I said, your help was appreciated, but now you can enjoy the rest of your vacation time."

* * *

Lance wasn't much of a drinker; he preferred being in control of all his faculties and decisions. Yet he sat at the end of the bar next to his motel and downed his second Jack & Coke. Sending Callie on her way had been difficult. Tougher, actually, then he would've thought it could be. It'd been a mistake to involve her in this op, not really knowing how dangerous it would potentially be. When he met her, it seemed like fate or something like it had dropped a beautiful helping hand in his path – well, after he'd figured out that she wasn't part of the opposition.

When Daughtry shared a message indicating that Cooper and his co-conspirators were preparing for some major increase in activity, and then he'd found the warning stabbed into the tree...

It didn't matter that she'd agreed of her own volition. That her boss at Infinite Security agreed. Better for her to be mad at him than to be hurt because of him.

Chapter 18

Callie

Less than three hours after she'd silently gotten out of Lance's vehicle and walked around the building to her own, Callie was still fuming. She gritted her teeth and tossed her suitcase into the trunk with enough force that it bounced against the side wall of the interior and pushed the emergency roadside assistance and duffel bag into the corner. It felt good. So good she wanted to yank her suitcase out and whip it in there again.

Vacations were supposed to be relaxing. A chance for rejuvenation, exploration, excitement, whatever you wanted them to be. Blah blah blah. This misguided vacation had been anything but relaxing.

She pulled the driver's side door open with equal force, anger and frustration battling with each other for position at the top of her emotional pileup; disappointment was running a close third. It took multiple tries to jam her seatbelt in the slot, the clanking noise each time adding to her aggravation.

No, it wasn't her investigation. Not her mission, not her op, not her anything. She just happened to be in the right place at the right time to stumble into Lance's case. Callie rested her forearms on the steering wheel and forced herself to breathe more evenly. It wasn't safe to drive when she was so... whatever she was.

Like Lance said, he didn't want or need her there. It was all under control, and she should conclude her vacation in any way she wanted. Never mind that it clearly *wasn't* all under control because nothing was concluded or resolved. Never mind that she'd spent more than her originally planned vacation immersed in this.

Callie carefully followed the loop around her cabin and slowly drove down the exit road to the front of the property. She'd already checked out on the television screen in her room and reached through her car window to drop the keys into the slot of the conveniently positioned return box.

The B&B had been nice, and the restaurants she visited were good. There'd been no free time to explore anything else in the area, and that she regretted. Maybe she'd eventually come back--if she could put this behind her.

At the end of the exit road, Callie switched on her left turn signal. There was more traffic than she would've expected on a Monday morning, at least at this hour. It was later than typical rush-hour—but maybe the ebb and flow of daily life was different in this area than it was downstate.

When she joined the flow of traffic on the four-lane road, she tried to enjoy the passing scenery. Trees and flowers in early summer bloom, occasional stonewalls, gently sloping hills that gradually gave way to sharper turns that more steeply brought her down the mountain. There were deer crossing signs, and she fleetingly wondered how often wildlife actually crossed the roads. Callie tried to find a radio station but gave up after a few moments. The reception on her usual stations wasn't good here.

She wanted to know how the case would end, and if it would end anytime soon. She could probably find out, ask Dax to look into it. Maybe put a word in Tia's ear and get her to ask Dax. Boss Man respected his wife and always took her seriously. Or she could research it herself, but if she did that and Lance found out, well, no way she wanted him to think she actually *cared*.

Trying to distract herself, Callie put on a playlist of upbeat music she'd curated for herself. Lance, with his gray eyes, confident swagger, skill on horseback, intelligent mind, and devastating kisses, could vanish into the mists of time like the age of the Renaissance did.

Disappointing, but she'd get over it.

Gradually, the roads widened as it continued the twists and turns that led to the point where New York roads crossed into New Jersey. Callie was careful to pay close attention to the signage. She certainly didn't need any further aggravation.

Route 9 was a heavily traveled, commercial thoroughfare, lined on both sides by a huge variety of retail stores, warehouses, marketplaces, and eateries. She hadn't paid much attention to any of it on her way to her destination, except to stop for fuel. Now, though, Callie was feeling a hunger headache that amplified the one that she'd been developing from stress.

"At least I can take control of that," she muttered, pulling into the next parking field in front a row of businesses that included a diner at the end. There was one parking space open on the end of the row. A placard with an arrow on it pointed to a rear parking lot, but Callie instead maneuvered into the available space at the front, tight though it was. She grabbed her pocketbook, locked the car, and headed for the other end of the strip of stores.

Callie could smell the welcoming aromas of burgers, bacon, and other diner food delights. It was barely 10 o'clock in the morning – was it too early for a burger? Should she stick with scrambled eggs, bacon, and toast? Her eyes scanned the store windows as she passed them. A women's clothing store, one that looked expensive. A hair salon, its windows decorated with gilt-edged mirrors framing faceless hair mannequins. A Discover! store, each of its window displays full of beautiful, artistic and science-related pieces. Callie was four footsteps beyond that store's final window when her mind pointed out something she'd just seen; one of window tableaux was arranged on tables in front of a hanging wall tapestry like one she'd seen at the Renaissance Festival.

She stopped in her tracks. No doubt it was a mass-produced item. Even though most people wouldn't want something like that in their homes, it was beautiful, and there had to be some percentage of the public who would enjoy it. Callie turned and meandered back to the store window. She took a closer look at the tapestry, and the items displayed in front of it.

Goblets set with gems glittered in the sunlight. Surrounding them were dinner plates of glossy wood, and others of what looked to be hammered metal. A decorative vase full of flowers and a small figurine depicting a knight on horseback added to the collection.

It was full of decorative items, similar in overall theme to those in the tableau, which depicted a blue-and-white draped wallcovering, Grecian-style figurines, and a distinctly Grecian vase. Still, Callie's interest was piqued.

Hunger set aside, she instead veered back to the store entrance. When she pulled it open, a rush of cool, faintly scented air greeted her, along with faint sounds of a Muzak system. Together, the environmental ambience was welcoming and relaxing, and generated a feeling of something she couldn't quite categorize. Yet.

"Good morning! Are you looking for something in particular today, or seeing what you can *discover*?" The woman's friendly voice slightly accentuated the last word, the well-rehearsed greeting seamlessly integrated the name of the store.

Callie turned to the speaker, a neatly dressed brunette woman in her early or mid-40s. The asymmetrical haircut she sported accentuated her high cheekbones and gave her a modern edge.

Callie made herself smile in return. "Both, I think. The tapestry in the last window outside caught my eye, and I was wondering what else you have that I might like."

"I'm Alice, and I'd be happy to assist you. Those are from our Medieval Collection. All are fine reproductions and pieces created by Discover! artisans, inspired by other work from that time period.

Each piece can be displayed to work with any kind of decor, or help you create a themed collection in your own home."

"That's amazing."

Allie beamed. "Isn't it, though? Have you ever shopped Discover! before?"

"No, I haven't. I've heard of it, of course. Seen commercials, I think." Callie had really only seen maybe one or two ads for Discover! but wasn't going to say that. "I don't know why I've never stopped into a location before."

"It can be intimidating, because everything is so wonderfully wrought, but I promise there's something for every budget. Shall we start with what drew you in?" Alice gestured toward the back of the store. "Our Renaissance and Medieval section is this way."

Chapter 19

Callie

Callie walked out of Discover! more than two hours later with multiple shopping bags full of merchandise. Her mind was racing, and she wanted to run to her car, to Lance, but she kept her calm but pleased façade in front of Alice, the other two sales associates, and the several other customers in the store.

With more self-control, Callie strolled to her car and stowed the bags in the trunk along with her suitcase. Her resolve to not see or think about Lance again needed to be shoved to the side. He hadn't mentioned Discover!, but maybe it was a theory he hadn't bothered to share with her. Anything was possible.

She had to find out, and she wasn't doing it on the phone or via some intermediary. The man had brought her onto his mission team on his own, and he'd just as quickly yanked her off it on his own. He could damn well answer her questions the same way.

When Callie slammed the trunk closed for the second time that day, her stomach growled, loudly reminding her that she'd abandoned the diner plan she'd made just a couple of hours ago. Hunger pangs had been displaced by investigative excitement while in the store, but now that reprieve was apparently over.

Callie snapped on her seatbelt and started the car. She backed the vehicle out of the parking space and started looking around for the closest fast- food option. Across the busy road and down a mile or so, she could see the trademark golden arches. Was there anywhere McDonald's wasn't? Today at least, it was a welcome sight.

After she snagged a six-piece chicken nugget meal, Callie was on the road again. She didn't like to eat while driving, but she could feel the pressure of time on her back. She had to find Lance, show him what she bought, and tell him her thoughts about what was going on. In person. And she wouldn't let him shuffle her off without listening to what she had to say.

Nuggets and fries were easy enough to manage as she retraced her path back toward the Renaissance Festival. She skipped the dipping sauces, because dealing with that could be more of a distraction, and she had to pay close attention to the road. It wasn't a five-star meal, but the food was hot and quickly filled the empty space inside. The space in her stomach, at least.

Using the voice activation link between the steering wheel and her mobile phone, Callie called Lance. She listened as it rang four times and then rolled over to voicemail. When she reached the place where the road narrowed after the state roads crossed, Callie tried again.

This time, she left a message. "It's Callie. I need to speak with you ASAP. Please call me as soon as you hear this."

Traffic was heavier than she'd anticipated, even on the smaller roads, and by the time she reached the Renaissance Festival grounds, she was getting anxious to talk to Lance. If she was right about this theory, then there could be a lot more at stake than they had realized.

Chapter 20

Callie

Monday at the festival was nearly as crowded as it was over the weekend. It seemed that people who came to the area for the weekend squeezed in one more stop or made use of multi-day passes before they went home.

Lance would definitely be somewhere on the premises. After all, the jousting event was among the most popular attractions. Callie looked at the time again as she searched for parking in the closest field. The jousting exhibition would be going on now, if he was taking part in that today, and the big event would be in a couple of hours. Yes, he had to be here.

As she drove around the perimeter of the parking field, a uniformed attendant stationed at the break for the second row flagged her down. With his orange light, he signaled for her to turn into the row. Callie raised her hand in thanks and followed his direction. Sure enough, a minivan was driving the other way out of the row on its way to the exit. She swept into the now vacant spot and shut down her vehicle.

Before she exited the car, Callie called Lance again. This time, he answered on the second ring, his voice clipped. The man managed to sound annoyed in just one word.

"Hello."

"It's Callie." She knew the self-identification was unnecessary, even as the words left her mouth.

"I figured. What do you want?"

"Lose the attitude," she told him, with equal bite. "I'm calling because I need to, not because I want to."

In the background, she could hear loud voices and sounds that made her think he was still amongst horses.

"I can't talk now, around people. You know that. It'll have to wait 30 minutes," Lance said and then he was gone.

She certainly wasn't going to cool her heels waiting in the car for a half-hour or until he got around to calling her back. Callie looked around. Much as she hated leaving everything she bought in the trunk, there was really no alternative. On her previous visits to the festival, she'd noticed that they rarely allowed packages into the fairgrounds. The board with rules had explained the exceptions to that policy, and she was damn sure that bringing in evidence that terrorist sympathizers were dealing dirty on the premises wasn't one of them.

This time, Callie didn't bother waiting for the shuttle bus. She fast-walked along the now familiar pathway to get to the front entrance of the festival. Fortunately, the ticketing line she chose was moving rapidly and she was through the gates in less than 20 minutes from when she hung up the phone.

Lance would no longer be on the jousting field for the exhibition. He had to be either walking around, or in the staff area. Grateful for a good sense of direction, Callie headed toward the staff area by the way the main thoroughfare. She also called him again. This time he answered on the first ring.

"You don't listen, do you?"

"Not when it's important to *not* listen," she retorted. "Like I told you on the phone, I don't want to talk to you, I *need* to talk to you."

"Where are you?"

"Passing the merchant areas, between that and the turn-off path to the walkway for the pub." Callie hesitated. "Should I wait for you here?"

"Yeah." From the sound patterns around him, she could tell that he was moving quickly.

She was anxious to meet with Lance, but traipsing about in search of him was much more inefficient than waiting for him at one stationary spot. That was usually good advice whenever one wanted to be found – but it required battling her own impatience, which wasn't an easy task.

Whatever he saw on her face or heard in her voice, nodded as if he finally understood her urgency. He grabbed her hand. "Come with me."

He took off at a pace that had her stumbling after him until she caught on. Some 30 steps away he paused and spoke quietly to another staff member, who nodded at him and smiled at Callie. Callie didn't even bother asking what Lance told the young man, because it didn't matter anyway.

All that mattered was sharing her thoughts with him and deciding what to do then.

Chapter 21

Lance

Callie didn't ask where they were going, she just kept pace with him and his longer legs. He glanced to his side, glimpsing her face as she scurried to keep up with him. Lance was aware that striding along this way was an asshole move, but that didn't slow him down. If she had the same hurt look on her lovely face that she did at the farm stand, he might backpedal and apologize, invite her back into everything, and he couldn't do that. Wouldn't do that.

When he reached a secluded area, although not the one where she'd first seen him with Eckert, Lance finally stopped walking.

"What is it?" His tone was curt and angry.

"Cooper and whoever his co-conspirators are, they are involved in something way bigger than Renaissance Festival antiquities rings." Callie took half-step closer to him. "I just came from a Discover! store, down on Route 9." She was speaking quietly but dropped her voice even lower. "In addition to carrying all different kinds of medieval replicas, the chain carries American Revolutionary war, Greek, Roman, Asian, and Middle Eastern merchandise." The intensity of her tone at her almost vibrating with excitement. "The helpful sales agent told me the company is so expert in selecting pieces to replicate for home use because they have an elite division that handles the real deal—real antiquities."

He didn't doubt for a moment that Callie was telling him exactly what happened, but still he asked, "She actually *said* that?"

"In those exact words," Callie confirmed. "She's proud of the company's expertise. As a store manager, I bet she has no idea what else that expertise can be used for."

How had he and his team not known this? Lance scrubbed one hand through his hair, and then the other, aggravation and agitation riding hot on each other's heels. He thought out loud, "Then why involve the Renaissance Festivals? Why take additional risks?"

"I've been asking myself that since my encounter with the store manager," Callie said. "Maybe it's just easier for them to handle individual, big ticket transactions that way."

"Involving an outside person doesn't make sense," Lance countered. "McKendrick came up clean. The guy wants us to clear his company of all involvement in this."

Callie admitted, "I don't know." She fixed him with a glare of her own. "Now you understand why I needed to talk to you."

He did understand, and it increased his worries about Callie more than tenfold. He had to tell her what was going on, on his end of things, and there was no easy way to do it. Lance squared his shoulders and prepared to rip off the Band-Aid, so to speak.

"There was a threat against you," he told her, with no preamble. "Delivered on a scroll jammed into a tree with a bloodied dagger." Her shocked face gave him no satisfaction. "The tree was in the clearing where I met with Eckert. The same spot where I then met with you."

Her next question was a quiet one. "If it was in that spot, then they know the truth about you."

"Something about me, at least." Lance looked around the perimeter again. "They might be fishing for intel. Might have suspicions but aren't sure."

"Still, not good." Callie frowned. "What was the threat about me?"

"It didn't specify you by name or exact description," he said. "It was a deliberately vague warning against "partners"."

She looked around them as she stated the obvious. "You have other people on your team here, not just me. I'm not even going to get into the chauvinistic way you booted me without telling me the actual facts, like you would have for a man on your team."

Lance cringed internally at her accurate accusation. She wasn't wrong, and he knew it. But he certainly couldn't tell her that his normal, level head was knocked off kilter by her. That his cool focus was rendered totally unfocused by her. By concern for her.

Lance respected women's skills, competencies, and professional acumen. He didn't think they needed to be wrapped in protective swaddling and placed on a high shelf for safekeeping. So why did he want to do exactly that with Callie? He ran a hand through his hair, agitated at the situation and himself. Was it just because they'd been intimate together?

He'd caused this when he gave into his attraction to her and breached the line between professional and personal. Lance didn't think there was any way of expressing that without hurting her or infuriating her.

Maybe both.

"You aren't with my company, and things changed from the situation I thought you were being brought in on." It was as close as he'd get to giving her an explanation. The truth of his reactions confused him but would likely – justifiably –piss her off. Lance hurried to add, "Make no mistake, I appreciate the insight you just shared."

"But you're still not going to change your mind about cutting me out."

"The facts that led to that decision have not changed," he said.

"Well, you have no authority over me. So, if I decide to spend the rest of my vacation time at the festival and in the area, that's purely my business. I may even decide to extend my time off." With that, Callie pushed past him and headed back the way they'd come.

Before she could get very far, Lance reached out and grabbed her arm. "You're supposed to be a professional, but you'll put yourself at risk out of spite or something?" He was incredulous, and didn't bother hiding it. "To prove whatever point you decided is so important?"

She rounded on him and poked him in the chest. "I caught the attention of a 'blonde woman' here, one that might've had eyes on Eckert and made him nervous enough to quit whatever he was doing for you. I never even had a chance to tell you that, and you never debriefed me before you cut me loose."

She was right about that, and he had no defense for it. "I became entirely focused on keeping you safe, which I admit wasn't in the best interests of the op." It was also incredibly embarrassing, but he wasn't going to go there and say so. "Tell me what happened with her."

Callie exhaled dramatically and once again parked her hands on her hips. "I was surveilling merchant booths and crossed paths with her several times. She spoke to me over knight on horseback figurines. She was cryptic, vaguely threatening, but not exactly. Then she took off and I couldn't find her again."

"What did she say, exactly?"

"Something along the lines of the festival being more dangerous than it appeared to be." Callie paused. "The whole time I was working my way through the merchant booths and tents, I couldn't shake the feeling that I was being watched."

"Well, it sounds like that woman could've been the one watching you."

"I'm sure it wasn't *just* her."

"Whoever is handling this for Cooper isn't doing it alone." He paused. "If there's some kind of connection to Discover! stores, this could be a much bigger operation than we first thought."

"Good luck with all that. It doesn't involve me anymore, remember?" Again, Callie turned to go.

And again, Lance reached out to put his hand on her arm. She wasn't going to make this easy, was she?

"I'm sorry my instinct was to protect you."

"Is that supposed to be an apology?" Callie turned to face him again. "That's a non-apologetic, passive-aggressive, deflection and justification combination crap unworthy of me or you."

This time when she started to walk away, he dodged around in front of her and blocked her path. She stopped moving. She planted her feet but softened her knees, adopting a casual but ready stance. "Lance, unless you are planning to test my hand-to-hand combat readiness, I suggest you get out of my way."

"I have no doubt about your abilities and no desire to test them," he assured her. "I just want to finish our conversation and apologize."

"No need to challenge yourself that way."

"It's not a challenge." As he said it, Lance realized he was gritting his teeth. He consciously relaxed his jaw and tried again. "I'm sorry I acted in a way that made you feel disrespected. That was not at all my intention."

"Now I'm curious," Callie said. "What *was* your intention?"

"To keep you safe when I became aware that the danger level was more than I realized when I brought you on board. I wouldn't have knowingly exposed you to that, especially without fair warning."

"You couldn't warn me about dangers you weren't aware of, could you?" Her statement was a reasonable one, delivered in a calm voice. It irritated him.

"We should have been aware. *I* should've been aware."

"You based your decision on the knowledge you had at the time."

Great, now she was making excuses for him and his high-handed behavior. He certainly didn't need her to do that; he'd take responsibility for his own Neanderthal behavior.

"I regret removing you from the team based on my own error in judgment. Would you be interested in rejoining the op?"

"If you'll consider my input and thoughts as seriously as you do anyone else's, then yes, I'd like that."

Lance offered her a firm handshake. "Agreed."

Callie cautioned him. "We have a lot to talk about before I can go forward."

"Also agreed regarding that."

"Tonight?"

"Tonight."

Chapter 22

Callie

The B&B had already rented out the cabin she'd been staying in, but one further around the bend was available and Callie was more than happy to take it. The layout was almost identical to the first one she'd had, but this one boasted a bigger bathroom with a bigger tub. It also had sliding doors to a rear deck with a wrought iron café table and two matching chairs. She might have enjoyed relaxing out there, if she hadn't gotten herself caught up in the intrigue surrounding the Renaissance Festival.

Not that she regretted it. Not really. And she didn't regret meeting Lance. Yes, his ridiculous protectiveness had infuriated her, but she didn't think he meant it to be demeaning to her or anything like that. For all he said to the contrary, she wasn't sure the man truly understood the extent of her abilities and capabilities. He didn't seem to realize that she wasn't in need of protection simply because she was a woman. Well, protection beyond the usual standard of someone having her six. Everyone needed *that*.

Fortunately for him, she didn't believe in holding grudges, and the case intrigued her. Plus, she found him ridiculously attractive. No wonder she'd ended up sprawled over him and under him in her bungalow. Thinking about it made her so warm she suspected there was a blush staining her cheeks. With both hands she pushed her hair back from her face and sternly ordered herself to get back to business.

Callie had her laptop on the kitchen table, a notepad open next to it. She'd filled at least two and a half pages with notes and thoughts about what was going on connected with the festival and Lance's investigation.

When the knock on her door came, Callie was ready for it. She peered through the peephole and recognized Lance on the other side, even though she'd unscrewed two of the three light bulbs that illuminated the little front porch.

She opened the door and ushered him in, then closed and locked it behind him.

Lance unzipped his windbreaker. "One of the lights outside isn't working," he said.

"I unscrewed a couple of the light bulbs."

"You unscrewed... Why?"

She could hear that he sounded genuinely perplexed. "I didn't think you'd want anyone potentially recognizing you, do you, what with things evidently getting more intense?" Callie asked and followed that with another question. "Water? Coffee? I don't have much to pick from."

He followed her into the small kitchen area. "Nothing for me right now. I made sure I wasn't followed and left my car in visitor parking in the rear of the main building, but you're right, I don't want that."

"There you go," she said, knowing that he now understood that she'd intentionally helped him out with her efforts. "I left enough light for you to not be totally in the dark, but not enough to help someone identify you."

"Good thinking."

She leaned her hips back against the kitchen counter. He braced his legs hip width apart and rocked back slightly on his heels. Callie refused to break the uncomfortable silence that settled between them. She wasn't in the wrong and although she was willing to put it behind them, that didn't mean she had to be the one who made peace first. Silence was a powerful weapon when dealing with difficult interrogations, petulant coworkers, and recalcitrant knights.

After a couple of silent minutes that felt like much longer, Lance spoke first. "As I told you before, I'm sorry for the way I handled our conversation at the farm stand."

Callie turned toward him. "You made that clear, and I agreed to let it go. We don't need to cover that again. But like I said before, if I'm going to continue to work with you, we need a new under-standing."

She couldn't quite identify the expression on his face when he said, "Are you saying you have a list of demands?"

"I wouldn't call them demands. Now I'm curious, though. Do you have a problem when teammates make demands of you? Or only when female teammates do that?"

Lance took two steps closer to her and spoke with an intensity she hadn't expected. "Look, just because you see me undercover as a medieval character doesn't make me a misogynistic dick. I treat female teammates the same way I expect them to treat me. With respect. And that usually means no one makes *demands*. We work as a team, carry out our missions, and fulfill our roles on each one as designated." He paused. "I'm team leader on this assignment. I thought you could help. I believe in your skill set. The threat level increased, and that's why I pulled the plug on your participation."

Callie held her ground physically, but her voice softened. "And you changed your mind again?"

"Yes. But with conditions. If you agree to them." Lance ran a hand through all his hair, leaving it in disarray. He slipped his hands into his pockets, then pulled them out and parked them on his hips. A second later he had them in his pockets again. Was Mr. Bossy and Sir In Control uncomfortable right now?

Callie moved around him and took a couple steps to the refrigera-tor. She passed him a bottle and took one for herself. Without discussion, they sat across from one another at the square wooden table. He set his bottle down on the red plaid runner that stretched across the small surface. "Full disclosure, one reason I believed in your skill set was my conversation with Daxon Meade at Infinite Security."

Callie started to speak, but Lance held up a hand to stop her and said, "It has nothing to do with gender. With him being a man and I believe him more than I did you, or anything like that."

She couldn't help it; she snickered at that. "I knew you checked with my boss, who happens to be a guy. That's not bias; it's just the facts."

"Again, I'm not trying to be a jerk or anything, I just want to make sure our cards are on the table. No secrets."

Although she appreciated the sentiment, Callie still intended to keep one secret: the ridiculous attraction she felt for her temporary team leader. She hadn't noticed any sign that he was attracted to her that way. There were no heated glances, no not quite inappropriate touches or innuendos tucked into their conversations. It sucked that her interest reciprocated, and she wasn't going to have time to try and seduce the man. Trying to do something like that wouldn't be smart anyway when she wanted to maintain her reputation as a professional.

With a start, she realized he was waiting for her to say something. "In the interest of clearing the air, Lance, I'm also not trying to be a jerk about things. As a woman in this type of field, a field dominated by men, I've had to learn to proactively stand up for myself."

"I get that. I also respect the hell out of it." He grimaced. "Please remember that when I tell you a few things I need you to do to make the mission at least a little safer."

It was obvious he was prepared for her to object to whatever he was going to say next. Callie leaned forward and took a sip of water, then replaced the cap on the bottle. "You have my attention, Lance. Don't keep me in suspense."

"Get a different car. I know it's a rental, so either swap it with them or return it and get one from somewhere else. We need to change your appearance. No one who sees you *isn't* going to remember you, so you need a wig or to dye your hair for the rest of the time you're here. Get some new clothes, maybe a new style or something. Anything to be less... you."

Callie couldn't be offended by his comment, even though she probably should've been. How could she be, when Lance was finally displaying things she'd been hoping for – clear signs of his attraction to her. The burning look in his eyes told her in no uncertain terms that he liked the way she looked right now – probably way too much.

And she liked that even more than she'd imagined she would.

Chapter 23

Callie

Mahwah, New Jersey was a short drive from the Renaissance Festival in New York – a mere 20 miles. Exchanging her vehicle there would give her the benefit of New Jersey license plates on a different vehicle, and that would help buy her at least a little time and temporary anonymity. Yes, her name would be in the electronic records of the car rental company, but (hopefully) no one would think to look for it.

After she returned her vehicle and paid all the fees for an out-of-state turn in, Callie was already tired of making nice with well-meaning people. The clerk at the counter of the rental car company couldn't fathom why she didn't just go the short distance to another of their locations over the New York border and avoid the surcharge. Callie made her excuses and left for the rival company conveniently located just two blocks away. There she paid the up-charge for an SUV.

Callie set her GPS for the beauty supply store in Spring Valley – which was back in New York. The welcoming storefront windows promised endless ways to make one more attractive and more confident. She pushed open the glass door and triggered a little bell hanging above it. The interior smelled invitingly of hair care products and body lotion, a combination more soothing than it sounded. She'd only advanced a half-dozen steps into the store before she saw what she'd gone there for. Shelves along one wall toward the rear of the store displayed the variety of wigs for sale. With single-minded purpose, Callie hurried over to them.

A young saleswoman appeared from around a display of nail care products. "Hi, I'm Katie. Do you see anything you'd like to try on?"

"Actually, yes, I do." Callie pointed at a brunette wig that interested her. "That one, I think." She decided to offer a reason for her interest in buying a wig. "Sometimes you just want a change."

"No problem!" With experienced hands, the sales associate retrieved the hairpiece from the wig form. "This is an excellent color for you, I think. It'll give you a different look, but it's not so dark that it will look off with your skin tone and all."

Katie escorted Callie to a private area with a long table set in front of an equally long mirror. The table was full of neatly organized combs, pins, setting sprays, hair sprays, and other styling tools. Callie watched as Katie deftly used a hairnet and bobby pins to corral her hair, then maneuvered the wig into place.

The transformation was immediate and startling.

Katie was quick to apply a darkening wand to Callie's eyebrows. She explained, "Your eyebrows don't need to exactly match your hair, but it's more natural if they are in somewhat the same color family."

"I see that you're totally right. It makes a big difference."

"Should I style it for you?" Katie asked, "Are you thinking this is what you're looking for?"

Callie met her eyes in the mirror. "I need to know the price, but I do think so."

"The cost of the wig includes the styling we are doing now, and a care kit that includes special shampoo, conditioner, a comb, brush, styling spray, and finishing spray." Katie beamed at her in the mirror. "Oh, and of course, a stand to put it on when you're not wearing it. Your new wig will look great for a long time, and you can always bring it back here to have it refreshed. I'll put the cost sheet in the bag."

The price made her own eyes widen, but she gave Katie the go-ahead and sat back as the wig was curled and styled in a casual, youthful way. When Callie was brought to the register, she decided to pay cash for the wig. No point leaving an easy trail.

On the way back to the town of Tuxedo, Callie stopped at a local strip mall. She was able to pick up new shorts, couple of new T-shirts, thin denim jeans, canvas tennis sneakers, and new sunglasses. All of the merchandise was rather cheaply made, but that made the price bargain-basement – and that allowed her to pay cash for it all.

When Callie drove away from the last store, in new walking shorts paired with a blue T-shirt, her new wig and new sunglasses firmly in place, behind the wheel of a different rental car, she was confident that she'd fly under the radar at the Renaissance Festival. For a few days, at least.

Callie made good time on her way back to where she needed to be. There was no point stopping at the B&B or anywhere else. She had what she needed, and her instructions; observe, observe some more, and gather any information she might be able to from those efforts.

Late in the afternoon, the lines at the gates were shorter than in the morning. People were adding on "pub crawl" tickets, which she'd already learned involved receiving an adult beverage from each of the two raucous establishments on the premises. This time, Callie also added a pub crawl ticket to her general admission.

Maybe she'd stumble across something more interesting than a bunch of drunken revelers.

Chapter 24

Lance

The view from atop his horse during the joust, and the routines that led up to it, gave Lance an excellent view of his surroundings. Better than he had when standing on the ground, that was for sure. His Renaissance Festival persona also allowed him to ignore most people, which was helpful in letting him focus on his own goals when enjoying that elevated perspective.

Sometimes, though, his cover of the job interfered. A trio of young women in the Dark Knight's section of the joust audience were enthusiastically waving at him, trying to get his attention. They stuck with their loud efforts long enough that he couldn't ignore them anymore. A key part of the festival job was to keep guests happy and entertained. He wasn't 100% sure his cover had been blown, and until he quit, he had to fulfill his festival responsibilities.

Lance directed Shadow toward where the women were seated – although they hadn't actually sat down at all. No, they were standing and jumping around and doing anything they could think of to get his attention. Those efforts included tying up their tight T-shirts to reveal more skin, creatively drawing open hearts with D. K. in them on faces and in cleavage and shouting sexually suggestive invitations at him. After raising a hand in greeting to a staff member dressed as a jousting assistant and getting that man's attention, Lance tossed him his helmet.

"Ladies." He sketched a bow on horseback, the reins loosely held in his left hand. "Did you find the joust good entertainment?"

"You were great!" The woman on the right was the only one who seemed capable of speaking to him.

The others were staring like it was his horse who decided to speak. "It was great."

"Everything was great. Especially you!"

It was both flattering and funny how they'd all been so bold in their efforts to get his attention, and then once they had it, didn't know what to do with it. He was deciding if he'd continue the conversation or end it there, when in his peripheral vision he glimpsed a solitary figure heading for the tree line—a tree line behind clearly posted notifications that the area was off-limits. Even festival staff wouldn't go that way.

Lance quickly made his excuses him to the women and whirled about on Shadow. He trotted over to the staff member who was assigned to the Dark Knight and lingering nearby.

"Kyle, I saw a visitor going into a restricted area, and I'm going after him." He swung down off the horse and tossed Kyle the reins.

Moving as quickly as possible, Lance started divesting himself of his armor.

Kyle used his free hand to help with the torso piece and assured him, "I'll get help stowing this. Call if you can't find the guy."

"Will do," Lance said, already taking off at a run in the direction he'd seen the man go. The sound of Kyle's voice faded behind him.

The trespasser hadn't even hesitated when he crossed over the warning line. Why wasn't he concerned about being seen? Or was his purpose so important that he didn't care? Lance knew exactly what was beyond that buffer of trees: electrical generators, water supply pumps, the control center for the on-site surveillance cameras, and other core components of the festival.

If the guy was supposed to be working back there, he'd have gone in the right way. And at the very least, he'd have been wearing something identifying him as staff– which he wasn't.

When he reached the tree line, Lance slowed almost to the point of stillness. He couldn't be absolutely certain where the guy had entered the trees, but there was no way he could be 100% sure. He scanned the ground, his sight line and slightly below of the bushes and trees, looking for anything that appeared to be recently crushed, impacted, or otherwise disturbed. When nothing caught his attention, Lance moved laterally to the left, continually scrutinizing the surroundings.

There was a pathway in this section, but the guy he'd see hadn't gone in by way of it. Either he didn't know it existed, or he had some other reason.

When Lance moved sideways again, he found what he'd been looking for – traces of a person having passed through recently. The groundcover was freshly trod. A couple of branches had snapped from being shoved aside. Along with the physical evidence in front of him, Lance could suddenly sense the presence of another person. He whirled around, prepared to fight and found himself facing Cooper— who had a gun pointed straight at his chest.

Cooper sneered. "So kind of you to accept my invitation, Dark Knight."

"The one you left pinned to the tree?"

"No, the one I gave when I strolled right by your section in the joust. I wondered if you'd be too focused on your fan club to pay attention."

Lance gestured toward the gun. "What's the point of this?"

Cooper moved toward him, forcing Lance to take several steps backward. "I find you amusing, but someone is tired of dealing with you."

From above and behind him, something hurtled to the ground, knocking Lance down and forward. There was just enough time for Lance to recognize that the something was a man before a hard object slammed into his head and everything went black.

Chapter 25

Callie

When Callie reached the jousting field, it was nearly empty. There were two horses being led by handlers, several people cleaning up debris left behind by spectators, and other staff performing tasks she didn't understand in the area where the jousting participants lined up with each other during the action.

One of the staff members called over to her. "This area is closed now, Miss." He pointed at the scheduled board by the entrance to the field. "The next exhibition is tomorrow at 1 o'clock."

"Thank you." Callie decided not to tell him that she already knew that. Her eyes were focused on the black horse with the one white lower leg. "This is Shadow, right? Lance's horse?"

"This is the Dark Knight's horse."

Of course, that would make sense. Lance had said it wasn't his own, personal animal. This horse was accustomed to having a rider wearing armor and participating in a joust. That had to be a learned skill for the horse as well as the rider.

There was no point asking where Lance was, because even if he knew, the groom was likely to give her whatever the standard line was in that situation. She'd just go back to the original plan about her exploring the premises as a visitor and observing things. Callie still didn't think that was likely to be productive, but she'd agreed... and that was that.

She left the jousting field behind and followed the wooden directional signs to the pubs. The sounds of laughter and partying got louder the further she walked along the indicated pathway. When the first pub came into view, Callie noticed that it faced other signs pointing the way to three particular merchants. It was probably smart to direct people who'd been drinking in the direction of places to spend money. It didn't escape her notice that one of the merchants listed was Modern Medieval, the company Lance had mentioned.

Even though it wasn't dark out yet, the first of the two pubs was well lit with fairy garden lights, as well as both individual candles and light fixtures fitted with candles, no doubt powered by electricity or batteries. The effect was warm and inviting, as was the laughter spilling into the air.

Callie made her way past visitors in contemporary clothing and people in attire that could pass as medieval or simply old-fashioned. Women in off-the-shoulder blouses and artfully rucked-up skirts swished between tables, delivering drinks and plates of food. When Callie slipped inside, it was easy to get lost in the crowd. She made her way to a spot near the crowded bar and fumbled in her bag for her ticket.

The barman scolded the two male customers in front of him. "Make room for the lady, you worthless pieces of dung."

They grumbled in mock offense, but still shuffled over in the to give her a few inches of space at the bar. She murmured her thanks to them and to the barman, who jabbed his thumb at the handwritten menu on the wall behind him and asked, "What'll you have?"

There wasn't much to choose from, so it was an easy decision. "Ale, please."

He pulled her drink from the tap, stamped her ticket, and turned to the next patron. Callie sipped from the plastic glass with "Renaissance Festival" emblazoned on it. The brew was surprisingly fresh and crisp, and it made her realize how thirsty she'd actually been.

For the next 30-some-odd minutes she wandered around the establishment before she went a little further down the path to the other pub. The styling was a little bit fancier, and wine was actually included on the bar menu, but it was essentially the same thing. In neither place did she find anyone engaging in clandestine conversation or anything remotely resembling suspicious behavior.

Callie pushed her cup aside in the second pub. At each bar she'd consumed less than half a cup, and at the second one had also eaten some excellent chicken tenders. Her head was clear and her body ready to continue, but she wanted to touch base with Lance. Although she'd texted him twice and called him once, he never responded to her messages. Was there any point in reaching out again? Maybe he was busy, handling something to do with the investigation and couldn't respond to her at the moment.

She blew out a heavy breath. She'd agreed to be a team player and follow his lead on the op. Her whole morning had been spent doing as they'd agreed with the car swap, the wig, the clothing. If he needed to speak to her, he'd reach out. Meanwhile, she just have to continue doing what she was tasked with doing.

Her final task for the day was to pay another visit to the merchant area, just to scope it out during the late hours of the day. Callie checked the time on her phone. There was slightly over an hour until closing. She'd do a quick walk-through then head back to the B&B. Hopefully, Lance would show up at her door again.

Callie left a generous tip on the bar and headed out the door. Plenty of people still wondered the paths, enjoying any last activities or entertainment they could fit into the day. When she reached the main shopping area, it was much more crowded than she expected. Now familiar with the layout and the merchants, she paid even closer attention to some of the specific merchandise and to Modern Medieval. The owner of the business had been cleared and was cooperative, but some of the illegal transactions had still passed through it.

If the owner had been clueless before, how did they know he wasn't still out of the loop on what was happening under his own nose?

With the number of people who came through the Renaissance Festival each day, Callie hadn't been at all concerned with anyone recognizing her as a repeat visitor. But since Lance was particularly worried about it, and she made the changes he required, she was now confident and comfortable that she appeared to be a first-time visitor.

In the booth with the floral designs, Callie purchased a hair clip she'd admired on a previous visit. Next door, in Modern Medieval, she wandered down the aisles. At the turn of the second one, a serving bowl with a mosaic caught her eye. She picked it up carefully, studying the inlaid pattern. It was lovely and familiar, because she'd admired it at Discover!

Callie heard the woman approach before she spoke. "Beautiful, isn't it?"

"It certainly is," she agreed.

"Are you a collector?" the woman asked.

"Of the real thing? I wish." Callie smiled at her. "For now, at least, I have to satisfy myself with reproductions." She nodded toward the bowl in her hands as she put it back on the shelf. "This is a lovely one."

"It is." The sales associate backed up a step. "Okay, well, let me know if I can help you with anything." She turned around moved towards front of the tent to assist another customer.

Callie frowned and continued her perusal of the items on display. There was no rational reason for the disappointment she felt. It wasn't like the woman was going to confide the company secrets to her – "Want to buy a true collectible and help fund some terrorists? Here's how we can help you do it..." If the salesgirl even had a clue about any of that, which she undoubtedly did not.

An older woman brought some kind of tabletop figurine up to the register. A couple who'd been examining framed prints left without buying anything.

Callie meandered around the last row of merchandise, which left her close to the rear entrance. She was two steps away from it when the man's voice outside caught her attention.

"– to you here and the buyer will be here two hours later."

"I thought he's taking a break?"

"This is too important. Just make sure you're here for it."

The men's voices faded a bit and Callie hurried outside. Two men stood nearby in close conversation. One had on the uniform for the store she just exited. She pretended to look for something in her handbag, hoping to hear more. Instead, the salesman was heading back into the shop, and the other man was walking away. Before she stopped to think about any reason why she shouldn't follow, Callie was doing exactly that – following.

Chapter 26

Callie

Callie pretended to be talking on the phone while she followed along behind the second man. She wanted to call Lance, leave a message if she needed to, but couldn't take a chance that her words would carry in the night air. It was better to carry on a fake conversation that would be good for him to overhear.

Her prey headed toward the exit. She told her imaginary friend on the phone that she was leaving the Renaissance Festival and would call her later. Callie's mind spun with ideas about how she could somehow follow this guy, which meant getting her car from the parking field and locating him again. Worst case scenario would be if he was parked in the small amount of spaces near the entrance.

He wasn't.

She joined him and five other people, two of whom had a young child with them, at the shuttle stop. Callie busied herself looking through her handbag and the bag from the floral design shop. She had mace and pepper spray, a folding knife, and a multitool, but that was not much to provide assistance in a physical confrontation. She was confident she could hold her own fairly well, but it would be nice to have more of a weapon if she needed one--especially if she was outnumbered.

She didn't expect anything like that to happen tonight. But her training taught her to be wary and be prepared.

When the shuttle bus to the parking fields arrived a few minutes later, she joined the others in climbing aboard. Her quarry sat in the first row behind the driver. Callie chose a seat two rows behind him and across the aisle.

She looked out the window but kept her eyes on him through the reflection in the glass now that night had fallen. She mentally catalogued her impressions of him. Average height, average weight, brown eyes, brown hair. No distinguishing features. Unremarkable clothing. Nothing that attracted attention or stood out in any way. The ideal type of person to get things done when you didn't want anyone to notice what was being done.

The shuttle entered the first lot, where there were two stops. At the first one, and the man she was following stayed on the shuttle. Callie gave a mental fist pump. She was glad she paid attention to the layout of the parking fields on previous visits. The second shuttle stop in field one was close to the start of field two, where her car awaited. She hoped he was in field two, as well. When he stood as they approached the second stop at the back of field one, that hope was dashed. No one else got off the shuttle at the same time, so she didn't get to watch him walk to his car. Still, she craned her head, trying in vain to see where he went.

When the shuttle bus entered the second lot, Callie was already poised to exit. The door was barely open when she pushed through. She ran to her new rental vehicle, key fob in hand, and threw herself into the front seat still wearing her cross-body and clutching the paper shopping bag. Putting her seatbelt on as she pulled through the empty space across from her, her eyes were already focused on the exit.

In many recreational parks, there was a glut of visitors leaving at closing time. Here, either the ebb and flow of attendees was different, or maybe that final surge was still to come. Parking fields one and two were still approximately half full.

The design of the parking fields fed everyone out the same two-lane exit, which ended up with an option to turn left or right onto the main thoroughfare. On the approach to that point of decision, Callie tried to figure out which car in front of her carried the man she was attempting to follow. Not the minivan with the stick figure decals on the back window indicating a family of five, a dog, and cat. He was unlikely to be the luxury car up ahead in the next lane. A guy striving to look average wouldn't want to stand out with a car like that one. She eliminated the bright red Jeep for the same reason. A few of the other vehicles had multiple passengers visible to her, so she ruled them out. That left her with two possibilities.

She was going to have to pick one or the other if they went in different directions. If she was lucky, they'd both go the same way.

Despite her silent prayer, crossed fingers, and repeated invocation of "please, please, please," the first of the two cars turned left and the other turned right. Her turn was quickly next. Callie turned left, in the direction that led away from the town where she was staying, the town closest to the Renaissance Festival.

Now she had to figure out if she was chasing the right car. If not, she needed to turn around and go the other way before she had no chance of catching up to him.

Here, the road was two lanes in each direction, although at some points it narrowed to one. Lighting was also minimal. The lane paint was luminous, and reflective markers were periodically affixed to the road and its borders. Lights glowed at long intervals along the expanse of roadway and at businesses scattered occasionally along its length.

Callie stayed focused on the car in front of her, and the one in front of *that*, which was her goal. The speed limit on the road bounced between 40, 45, and 55, with the occasional dip down to 30.

A quintessential speed trap set-up. She'd have to balance the need for speed and the need to stay on the right side of the law.

With her eyes laser focused on the road and drivers ahead, Callie was aware of the miles clicking. The darkness quickly deepened, reminding her they were far from a city of any size. At last, the driver of the car directly in front of her signaled his intention to turn. When he was out of the way, Callie steadily closed the gap between her car and that of the man she was following.

Two more miles clicked by. Five more miles. Another five miles. When the other driver left his blinker off but angled right onto an off-ramp, Callie didn't hesitate to follow, although she used her turn signal. If he was paying attention in his rearview mirror, she didn't want him to know for certain she was following. Failing to signal would make her path feel impulsive, not intentional.

At the end of the off-ramp was a traffic light with a "No Turn On Red" sign. Callie feigned refreshing her lipstick in the visor mirror, trying to look casual. She took care keep her face obscured as much as possible behind the thick shield. She still saw when he made the right turn even though the light was still red.

Callie threw her lipstick on the seat next to her. She inched her car forward to check for oncoming traffic and then quickly made the turn. Like before, she focused on eliminating space between them. There were stores set widely apart on both sides of the road, and traffic was sparse at this hour. Everything was closed for the night, except an outpost of a fast-food chain whose iconic logo beamed its crown into the sky.

Another few miles went by. They passed what looked like an office building. A warehouse. A lumberyard. Another warehouse. A lot full of parked yellow school buses. Another warehouse. It still took her by surprise when the car in front of her made an abrupt turn into the parking lot of a big building with a sign that read "P & M Global." She drove down to the next building and into their empty parking lot.

A quick Internet search for P & M Global resulted in written doublespeak that seemed to indicate it was a manufacturer of some sort. What was that guy from the Renaissance Festival doing here, long after business hours, at a building that was dark?

Whatever it was, it certainly wasn't good. She didn't need her churning instincts to tell her that.

Once again, Callie called Lance. Once again, there was no answer.

She quickly dialed Dax. He answered on the second ring. "Callie. Surprised to hear from you this late."

"I've been tracking a suspicious person since he left the Renaissance Festival and is now in a darkened building for a company that has no clear Internet presence." Callie kept an eye on her rearview mirror in case anyone were to approach. "I haven't been able to reach Lance since early this morning. We're supposed to be no contact during the day, so I wasn't concerned before, but he should have checked in by now."

She could hear Dax moving while they were talking and now she heard more voices. Dax told her, "I'm with Mason and Jace now. I'm putting you on speaker."

Callie quickly repeated what she'd told Dax so her other colleagues could hear. Then she said, "I dropped you a pin with my location. I'm going to approach the building. See what I can see."

"Is anyone from Lance's team on your six?" Mason asked.

"No. He's down two guys, and Golden is stretched thin right now. We were just observing, gathering intel." She dropped the pepper spray and mace into her pockets. Shoved the small knife into the top of her sock. "I called his on-site backup but didn't reach him either. Can you guys notify his office? Maybe he checked in with them."

Jace spoke up. "Pretty obvious somethings not right, Callie. You know you should wait for backup."

Callie found a home for the multitool in a pants pocket. "I'm just going looking. Not making contact," she assured them. Silently, she added, "Unless I need to."

When Dax spoke again, he was deadly serious. "You think something happened to Lance."

"Yeah," she admitted. "He wouldn't be out of touch this long otherwise."

Not when he was so worried about her safety.

Chapter 27

Lance

Despite the pain in the back of his head, or maybe because of it, Lance was acutely aware of the irony of the situation. He'd been so concerned about Callie's safety and here he was. He was the one who actually got bashed in the head and carted off like a sack of cement.

He'd woken up as a man finished securing him to the chair, another man standing close by but out of reach, with a gun pointed at Lance's head. Dizziness and the weapon kept Lance from fighting them off before he got his bearings. But those factors didn't stop him from flexing all his muscles while the other guy tied off the ropes. It was an old trick, but one these two clearly didn't know. After they both moved away and he relaxed his muscles, all the ropes were significantly looser. Lance shifted against the chair, earning himself even more slack.

He decided to behave in a way they wouldn't expect. Lance smiled and taunted them. "What are we doing here, guys? I'm already bored."

If he could throw them off their game, he might learn something useful--and keep his mind off Callie.

Nope. No chance of that happening. He was worried that they'd captured or hurt her, too.

The shorter of the two guys exchanged a glance with the other and jerked his head towards the far end of the room. After he received a sharp nod in return, he walked off in that direction. Lance watched him jam his pistol into his shoulder holster as he left.

The remaining tango looked at Lance. Said nothing. Looked away. He looked enraged, and Lance wondered why he didn't act on it. Instead, he took up a position leaning against the wall across from Lance.

"What's your name?" Lance asked. "Are you Grunt 1, and he's Grunt 2?"

Still no answer. Lance started working on loosening the ropes around his wrists even further. From the feel of it, it wouldn't take long to maneuver one of his wrists free of the binding. Once he did that, it would be a matter of seconds to free himself entirely. He could take the guard in less minute and a half.

A text alert sounded, and his silent guard checked his phone. Whatever he saw there had him straightening up and looking toward the door. There was the scraping sound of a metal door and then footsteps.

Tom Cooper appeared in the doorway. Even though the images they had of Cooper were not good, they were good enough that recognizing him was easy. After identifying Cooper as a buyer in an illicit antiquities' transaction at the festival, a goal of Lance's investigation had been to catch the suspected ringleader and confirm his active involvement – but not under these circumstances.

Cooper barely glanced at the man who obviously worked for him, his attention instead fixed on Lance. He was positively gleeful. "Not so fearless and strong now, are you, Dark Knight?"

Since Cooper was looking to engage, Lance remained silent.

Cooper tried again. "Now you've got no valiant steed or suit of armor to hide behind." Cooper moved closer, apparently confident that Lance was securely tied to the chair and couldn't hurt him. "I bet you're surprised, aren't you?"

When Lance still didn't answer, Cooper's gaze swung the guard. "How hard did you guys hit him, Simmons? He can't talk?"

Simmons shrugged. "He was talking okay a while ago."

"You're playing games with me?" Cooper snarled at Lance. "Big mistake." He backed up a few steps, still glaring at him, although his next words were for Simmons. "I'll be back. *Soon.* Don't take your eyes off him."

Simmons acknowledged the order, and Cooper stormed off. The scrape of metal and the sound of the metal door slamming shut echoed in his wake.

Chapter 28

Callie

Callie clung to the shadows that smothered the building. The exterior was poorly lit, so it wasn't difficult to do. The building was set a good distance back from the road so she wasn't concerned about a passerby sounding the alarm. She listened carefully, then tried to quiet her own breathing because it sounded way too loud in the silence. The only other thing she could hear were the quiet sounds of the occasional passing vehicle.

Still, Callie couldn't let her guard down. Staying as tightly as possible against the brick building, she inched her way along its north side. Chain-link fencing with privacy strips woven throughout shielded the side of the property. She was at least halfway down what she perceived to be its length when she heard the muffled sound of boots on the ground. Her progress halted. Callie canted her head in the direction of the sound. It had to be coming from the rear of the building. She frantically looked around but couldn't make out anywhere to take cover. The building was low, relatively speaking, but she couldn't make out visible handholds that would allow for a vertical ascent. There were windows, but they were above her height.

She could feel her adrenaline rise as she prepared to either run or fight.

It took a moment for her to realize that the wearer of the boots was walking away from her direction.

Callie continued her path along the side of the building. When she came to the corner, she peered around the back edge. Here, two lights mounted on the bricks illuminated what had to be a doorway. On the far side of the doorway, she could make out the outlines of dumpsters with debris piled up next to them. There was an expanse of ground behind the building. From the glow of the lights, her best estimate was that it was at least 25 or 30 feet to the perimeter fence. Chain-link. The same as on the side of the building.

Heart pounding, Callie continued to make her way along the rear wall of the building. Cigarette butts dropped on the ground beneath a small awning-like overhang indicated where the wearer of the boots had been posted. Was he a security guard? Was this a legitimate business after all?

Hurrying as much as she could, Callie scanned the rear of the building. There was a window on one side of the back door, before the dumpsters, and a single bay loading dock on the other. The window was lower than the ones on the side of the building. She pressed herself up on tiptoe to peer through it. There was a light on inside, but it seemed to be coming from an area beyond the space closest to where she was looking from, and she couldn't make out anything in between.

The heavy footsteps were returning. One set, like before, but he was speaking now, so he had to be on his phone. He was speaking English, but with a Middle Eastern accent of some kind. Inwardly Callie cursed the fact that she was so bad at differentiating one language from another – at least in verbal form. She might have had some success if the words were written or if she had a lot of time, but neither was the case. She was screwed. She couldn't go back the way she'd come, or she'd run right into the guard. Going forward altered nothing if there were only windows, like there was on the other side of the building.

Callie looked up. If she climbed on a closed dumpster, she had a chance of reaching the edge of the roof overhang and pulling herself up.

Before she could make even a hurried risk-benefit analysis, Callie was already scrambling onto the closer of the two dumpsters. She tried to tune out the sound of the guard's approach and focused on grasping the edge of the roof overhang. There was no time to plan the best way to do it; she was on her belly on the roof edge before she could figure out how to accomplish it.

"Soon, he says. They will be here soon," the guard said.

Callie worked to control and quiet her breathing so she could focus on the audible half of the guard's conversation.

"I don't know."

She heard the soft sound of him striking a match to light another cigarette. "I don't care. Not my problem."

He laughed, but it was a humorless sound. "I get paid the same no matter what I have to do, even being a cleaner."

She didn't know *who* was going to be arriving soon, or how fast "soon" would be. She didn't know how to get inside that building to find out how—or if!—the guy she followed was connected to the Renaissance Festival and Modern Medieval. This guard wasn't being particularly attentive to the building or anything else. That probably meant nothing much was going on. Yet.

It was that, or he was incredibly lazy. Either way, she still needed to see what was going on inside. If more people were really on their way, could she waste time trying to figure out a covert way to enter?

No.

Callie looked around the rooftop area closest to her, trying to figure out something – anything – she could use as a weapon. Sure, she had her small knife on her, but to use that she needed to use it on this guy very accurately in a way that would probably kill him, and she didn't know if he was really a bad guy or just some real security guard who had no idea about the kind of people he was mixed up with.

That was an unlikely scenario with the way he talked about being "a cleaner," but it was still possible.

She crawled on her hands and knees several feet to one side, searching. Nothing. Callie stopped, listening again for the rumble of the guard still speaking on his phone. *Was he done already?* No, but now he sounded aggravated.

Well, so was she.

Until she wasn't, because she found a short stack of bricks at the corner of the roof. They were real, and similar to those that comprised the building itself. Repair work must have been done at some point, and they were left behind.

She had to figure out how to jump down from the 10 to 12-foot height of the overhang area onto the guard, and bring the brick with her. Her mind spun with possibilities until she decided the only real option was to hold the brick in her hand. She shoved an extra one in a utility pocket of her pants and gripped the first in her hand, adjusting it as best she could to hold it tight.

Callie stayed low and crept as close as possible to the edge. Moving slowly, silently, she swung her legs over the lip and scooted forward. The guard had ended his call already, and she could see the red glow of his cigarette as he continued to enjoy it. She regulated her breathing, consciously relaxed her muscles, and jumped.

The guard must've heard something because he was turning to his right when she collided with his back. Her arm came up and introduces the side of his head to the brick still clutched in her hand. Callie expected him to shout, to cry out, but instead he crumpled soundlessly onto the concrete below them. The impact jostled her more than she had anticipated. Her body skewed to the left, and she barely kept from having her own face smashed into the hard surface below them.

Powered by adrenaline, Callie sprang up from the ground. She pressed two fingers to the side of the guard's neck, feeling for a pulse, grateful when she found it. She pulled off her own cloth headband and improvised a gag, twisting and knotting the baby blue fabric at the back of his head.

She needed to tie him up and figure out a way to hide him from being spotted with ease. Callie scurried to the nearby dumpsters, already looking for something she could use as makeshift restraints. She never even had to open the metal containers. Piled on the ground next to them were empty boxes and cut lengths of thin rope, probably from securing the boxes together. Intensely focused on the task in front of her, Callie efficiently secured the guard with his hands behind his back and his ankles tied together. She took an extra minute to run a rope from his bound ankles to his forearms. Done with that, she dug in his pockets for weapons and his mobile phone. Her search yielded a Sig Sauer P226 Legion with extra rounds, plus a lethal looking Buck tactical knife. She shut off his phone and tucked it in her own pocket.

Conscious of every passing second, she assessed the best way to move him away from the door. Tossing him into a dumpster wasn't feasible.

"Sorry, dude," she muttered when she grabbed hold of his feet and started backing up toward the dumpsters. She knew she was scraping his face on the concrete, but it couldn't be helped. There was no time to even move the dumpster away and hide him behind it. The best she could do was position him with his face to the wall and scatter the boxes and other debris around him, essentially burying him in trash.

The exterior of the building was still quiet. Callie stole another look through the window, but nothing had changed. She pulled on the handle of the door and was gratified when it opened silently. There was no way to know what she'd find on the other side. All she knew was that while she was praying it wouldn't be Lance, she was also expecting that it would be.

Chapter 29

Lance

Lance was listening to the sounds of the building around him, which was probably why he immediately sensed Callie's presence. At least, that's what he told himself. He pretended to be unconscious while he waited for Cooper's man to either leave or be distracted.

Distraction won the day. The guard took a nap.

Cooper's man dragged another folding chair from where several of them were clustered near Lance. He shoved it against the wall further down and on the other side of the room and flopped down heavily. Lance watched from beneath his eyelashes as the guy fidgeted. He moved his legs, rearranged his arms across his chest and then over his stomach, obviously trying to get comfortable. Simmons' body relaxed incrementally, and Lance patiently waited. He was prepared to do whatever necessary to escape the situation, but it was beginning to look like shockingly little would be necessary. When the first light snore reached him, Lance finally opened his eyes all the way and looked for Callie.

The large room in which he'd awakened was cluttered with wooden crates and shipping boxes. From his vantage point, he couldn't make out shipping labels with enough clarity to read addresses, if there were any. He didn't know if Callie was hiding amidst them or elsewhere in the building. There was a walkway around the second level that might be providing her with access to hiding places he couldn't see.

He couldn't call out for her and risk waking Simmons.

Noise from outside ended up preventing him from doing anything. He took a chance and said loudly, "Stay there!"

When Simmons startled awake, Lance played it off. "Really, just stay there. Don't bother waking up just because somebody's here."

Almost simultaneously, the door at the entrance to the building slammed open and multiple pairs of boots could be heard tromping into the outer room. Cooper appeared in the doorway, followed by a big guy kitted out in protective gear with a weapon lashed across his chest. On his heels was Robert McKendrick, followed by two additional heavily armed men.

"Are you fucking sleeping?" Cooper snapped at Simmons. "You lazy asshole!"

Simmons tried to shake off the last vestiges of slumber, but it'd been easily apparent from his slack expression that Cooper had it right. Simmons stumbled over his own words. "I wasn't –. I didn't –."

"Get outside. You're on guard duty with Kipling, you useless piece of shit!" Cooper sneered at him. "Move it!"

Simmons turned on his heel and took off across the room. Lance heard him slam through a door somewhere in the room past them. Meanwhile, he was still focused on McKendrick. The older man didn't appear under duress in any way. What the hell was the owner of Modern Medieval doing with Cooper? He waited for Cooper to reveal that, while he surreptitiously studied the armed men who'd come in with them both. These guys looked hardened in a way that Simmons didn't. Lance didn't know Kipling, but suspected Cooper's other man might be equally incompetent.

He didn't need to wait long.

Cooper stomped closer to Lance. "Let's pick up where we left off.

Who are you working with – and I don't mean your damn company. I want names."

"He's not going to give you that." McKendrick stepped forward. There was no trace of the congenial, slightly befuddled businessman Lance had met before. No, this man was angry and exerting a lot of self-control to contain it. "You had to keep digging. Keep pushing."

The back door slammed. Seconds later Simmons burst into the room. "Sir, I need to–"

Cooper spun toward him. "Seriously, jackass, do your fucking job!"

Simmons tried again. "I need to tell–"

"Do I need to use a bullet to fucking explain this to you?"

This time Simmons lifted his hands halfway into the air and then backed up two steps. "Sorry." He turned and left the way he'd come in.

Lance desperately wanted to know where Callie was hiding. He couldn't look around again. There were five sets of eyes on him, and he couldn't take that chance. He *wouldn't* take any chance with her safety.

Why was she here? Callie had given him her word that she wouldn't take unnecessary chances. Hell, that's why he'd had her change her vehicle. Her clothes. Her hair. It's why he stayed away from her at the festival today.

And she still ended up here, in the middle of a mess that was sure to get even messier.

Cooper crouched in front of Lance, trying to meet his eyes. "Really, man, why do you give a fuck about a bunch of old crap? I bet you don't collect that shit." Another humorless laugh. "It's none of your fucking business."

Lance leaned forward in his chair. He wanted to punch this guy in his traitorous mouth, but he couldn't. He couldn't reveal the fact that his bonds were so loose.

"You think you can funnel money to terrorists, and no one will care? You can get rid of me, but hundreds of other people will take over for me."

A flicker of confusion changed Cooper's expression. "What the hell are you talking about?"

McKendrick spoke up then. "It's just info my people planted. Don't worry about it. Don't get distracted."

Cooper stood up and faced McKendrick. "You're putting info out there that I'm a terrorist or something?"

Lance was more than happy to fill Cooper in on the facts. "The intel that you are actively raising money to support what they do. The bombings and the killings, that you agree with their tactics so much that you give millions to them."

"Don't let him get your head," McKendrick snapped at the younger man. "You've got nothing to worry about."

Lance hid the fact that his own mind was spinning, trying to put these new pieces in place. McKendrick was the actual architect of the black-market antiquities ring. Cooper was in on it but clueless about key parts.

"You make that much money off this scheme that it was worth it to you to create a whole set of lines around this guy?" Lance asked.

"Not your concern, is it?" McKendrick smirked at him. "Don't be embarrassed that you fell for it. Bigger fish have taken the bait."

"What's your connection to the Discover! stores?" Lance hoped that somehow Callie was hearing this. That she'd escape the building without anyone knowing, or stay hidden until they all left. He was sure they were going to kill him – or at least try to – but he wasn't giving up and accepting it yet. If necessary, she would get the info to the right people.

"What do you know about the Discover! stores?" McKendrick demanded, no longer looking smug. "Tell me!"

Cooper was no longer willing to shut up because McKendrick told him to. Evidently, finding out that your business partner had painted a target on your back to distract people was too much.

"He's got a network of smugglers, forgers, and thieves giving him real-deal stuff and top-notch fakes, and he replicates for the stores. He owns the stores, I don't know how he hides it from people, but he does." Cooper delivered his info dump at lightning speed, the words tripping off his tongue faster and faster.

McKendrick shouted at him, fury reddening his face. "Shut up, you moron. Shut the hell up!"

Cooper yelled for Simmons and Eckert, who were nowhere to be found. McKendrick started to give orders to the man who'd accompanied him but was startled into silence for a moment when Lance lunged forward in his seat, hands free and tearing at his ankles.

In the next instant, glass shattered, and a horde of modern knights burst through two doors and a window. Chaos ensued. As the men from Infinite and Golden quickly dealt with gunfire and attempted resistance in the main room, Lance raced toward the back.

"Callie, where are you? I know you're here!"

It was hard to hear over all the noise the men were making, but her voice rang out clear as a bell. "Up here! Lance, up the stairs."

He looked around frantically. There was a narrow staircase on one side of the room. When he ran over to it, he could see her at the top. Lance took the steps two at a time. There was an office area to the right, and to the left was the walkway he'd spotted from his position in the chair down below.

His eyes roved over her from top to bottom, desperate to make sure she was uninjured, and then simply desperate for her. She was wearing the dark wig she must've bought that morning, a short-sleeve blue T-shirt, and slim fitting black cargo shorts. The gun casually shoved into her waistband looked as natural as her smile when she saw him. Callie pushed up on the balls of her feet, and he met her halfway for an abbreviated version of the kiss they both wanted.

She took his hand and tugged him behind her onto the walkway so they could see the scene below. Four men were kneeling with their hands zip-tied behind their backs, under the watchful eyes of Jonathan, from Golden, and a huge guy from Infinite. Cooper was flat on his back, either injured or dead. Lance recognized his friend,

Jace, from Infinite. He had an injury of some kind on his upper body tended to by someone else. He was laughing at something the other man said, so Lance figured the injury wasn't serious. Two people were on their phones, including his colleague, Sean.

Callie bumped his shoulder. "Too bad you don't have a recording of the conversation with McKendrick and Cooper."

Lance put his hand on top of hers and squeezed it quickly. "Yeah. But I'm a witness, and if you heard any of it, so are you."

"There's that," she agreed. "There's also this." She held out her phone and played a recording for him of part of that conversation. Even though she'd been at a good distance from it, the acoustics of the space had significantly magnified the sound. It was sharp and clear.

Lance laughed silently. He slipped an arm around her waist and pulled her close. "You are definitely a woman of many talents."

"You don't know the half of it," she informed him with a wink.

So he kissed her again.

Chapter 30

Callie

She'd ordered hot chocolate after eating in the late dining area of the main building at the B&B. The building was cozy, but the frothy drink was a preemptive effort to combat the chilly night she'd be walking through to get back to her accommodations.

It turned out, though, that the real heat at the tiny table was coming from the presence of the Dark Knight seated across from her. Lance was wearing contemporary clothing now, of course. Somehow, his Renaissance Festival persona shone through the dark jeans and black Henley. He met her there for dinner because she'd be checking out the next day and heading back to Long Island.

She couldn't stop thinking about the night they were interrupted when he showed up unexpectedly at her bungalow. Callie said, "So, I was thinking. No, I guess I was wondering..."

Lance leaned across the table. He cut off the nervous stream of words coming from her lips with his own lips. The kiss was a delicious combination of demanding authority and coffee-warmed lips moving in perfect time. The sounds of the small café faded away. Callie parted her lips and invited him in. His low groan vibrated through every part of her.

When Lance finally drew back from her so they could both catch a breath, the whiskey fire that had ignited in his eyes warmed her skin even more. He kept his voice low. "Are we going to your cabin, or are we saying good night?"

Callie didn't hesitate. "Let's go."

The hot drinks had been complimentary, but Lance left money on the table to cover dinner before taking her hand to walk with her to the bungalow. The walkway to the rear buildings was well lit but didn't distract from the brightness of the moon and stars shining down upon them.

They'd reached the porch and Callie handed him the key so he could open the door. Lance ushered her inside and then closed and locked it with an economy of motion. As it had before, the furniture looked even more fragile in his presence. Neither spoke until they reached the bedroom. She was glad the four-poster bed looked solid.

He spoke softly by her ear. "I want to get you on that bed and find out exactly what you like, what you want, and how hard you need it tonight, Callie. I want to see you come undone for me." Lance nuzzled her jawline. "If that's not what you want, I need you to tell me now."

"Sounds perfect to me," she said, anchoring herself with her hands firmly on his shoulders. This wasn't the more tentative exploration they'd enjoyed here before. Between deep kisses and dirty promises, Lance had her clothing quickly stripped away. He was covering much of her exposed skin with sharp nips and hot, lingering caresses. The expression on his face showed that he appreciated the way her excited breath made her breasts rise and fall in response. Or maybe how hard her dusky pink nipples already were from pure anticipation.

Lance stepped out of his boots. He dropped his shirt, jeans, and socks to the floor, but his eyes never left her. Then his hands were on her again, touching and stroking, exploring and enticing. He nibbled and licked at the underswells of her breasts, traced delicate circular patterns around her nipples with his tongue. When his mouth closed over one, and then the other, she couldn't stop the sounds of pleasure that escaped. Callie wanted to tell him she knew they were small, but he made them feel so good... and she couldn't form the words.

Then Lance said, "A damn perfect mouthful."

The best response she could manage was a whimper that almost sounded like "Please."

Keeping her close, he backed her up to the bed and shoved aside the already turned-down quilt. He followed her down onto the crisp white sheets.

"Lie back, beautiful. Let me taste what I do to you."

Chapter 31

Lance

He didn't taste her. No, that implied something fleeting and almost casual. Lance devoured her instead, worshiping the treasure between her legs with intense focus and shameless desire. He listened to the frantic gasps of her breath, felt the sting of her fingers pulling at his hair, the press of her thighs against his face. When she fell apart beneath his onslaught, he savored every tremor as if it were his own.

Lance did his best to keep one hand touching her as long as he could while he reached for his jeans when they were crumpled on the floor. He retrieved a condom and returned to her side. Unhurried, he kissed her gently once, twice, then more deeply again, letting her taste herself on his lips.

Her back arched as she tried to get even closer to him. "I want you," Callie said.

Lance was too far gone to tease her, to edge her, to delay burying himself in her wet heat. He sheathed himself quickly, then hesitated.

"We didn't talk about personal history, but I can tell you I'm clean, always have been. Was tested four months ago and haven't been with anyone since," he said.

"Same here, but it was six months ago for me," Callie told him.

He wove his fingers through hers, firmly pressed the back of her hands against the bed. Lance slowly pressed his length inside her, feeling her pussy tightening around him more and more the deeper he went. A series of short, rhythmic thrusts brought him home to where he suddenly knew he belonged.

Callie wrapped her legs around him, arching even further toward him. She struggled to get the words out. "Lance, I'm so, mmm, close."

Lance released her hands and brought his back a bit to change the angle, grinding against her clit on each downward stroke. She ran her hand up his arms, scratching and grasping at his skin. Unintelligible words and sounds of pleasure filled the air along with the primal music their bodies were making. He gritted his teeth, trying to hold back his own finish until hers was complete. When she cried his name out again, Lance gave up on fighting a battle he couldn't win and filled the condom with his tribute to her.

An hour later, they were cleaned up and relaxing in the beautiful bed that had proved its worth. Lance lay with one arm behind his head and the other stroking Callie's hair where it spilled across his chest. He had something to tell her. Or to ask her. He was normally a very decisive person, and his current indecisiveness was wrecking this precious time.

"Callie, we need to talk."

She lifted her head to make eye contact. "That sounds ominous."

"Kind of depends on your reaction." Lance paused. "You know your colleague, Jace, is my friend from way back."

"Yes," she said warily.

"Jace tried to recruit me a year or so ago, but I was under contract with Golden. That contract is ending in a couple of weeks, and I'm seriously considering making the change."

She sat up further and pulled the sheet around her. "But now you're afraid I'm going to be a stage five clinger or something."

"I'm going to stop you right there," Lance said. "I want to know if you'd be comfortable with having a romantic relationship with a coworker."

He couldn't quite decipher the expression on her face. *Maybe she wasn't interested in pursuing this the way he was?* "I'm trying not to make you uncomfortable, so if you're not interested in that with me—"

Callie melted into him like butter on hot waffles. "Damn right, I'm interested." In an agile move she turned around and straddled him. "Consider me your personal welcoming committee."

About the Author

DENISE DEMARCO, a lifetime New York resident, often uses her knowledge of the tri-state area in her stories. Genealogist, researcher, history buff, and collector of information about anything and everything, she creates stories from the heart from all that—plus, lots of imagination and iced coffee!

Available Now

* * *

Chapter 1 – Liam

If the guys found out how he spent a rare summer day off, he'd never live it down.

Doing these things online was more convenient, but some-times Liam wanted to see with his own eyes what he was going to purchase, not have it filtered through a camera lens. In this case, handling matters 'in-person' was unavoidable.

Head down, sunglasses still on, Liam strode under the royal blue awnings with their crisp white lettering and into the building. In addition to the lights strategically positioned everywhere inside, sunlight streamed through the huge plate glass windows that spanned the whole first floor. Although they looked like regular windows, he knew they were crafted of a protective glass to eliminate harmful rays that might damage any of the valuable antiquities inside. As best he could tell without getting close to them in a way that would arouse suspicion, the windows were impact resistant as well.

The well-dressed man who greeted him was attired to meet expectations for the ritzy Park Avenue address in Midtown Manhattan. Liam had been here many times and was familiar with the layout already, but a certain level of procedural decorum was expected in these places. Hands loosely linked in front of him, the auction house representative still managed to grip a small tablet device. In-house communications, perhaps? The man's posture managed to be both relaxed and attentive, and he was friendly in a practiced, professional way.

"Good morning, sir, and welcome. How can we help you today?"

"Good morning," Liam said. "I'm here for the rare book auction."

"Excellent. There's quite a lot of excitement for that auction today. I'm Brett. I'd be glad to be of assistance."

Liam smiled politely, knowing full well that the same exact sentences were said to everybody who was there for an auction. Nothing here was personal, and he wasn't going to let the obsequious behavior distract him from his goal.

"Do you wish to review anything about auction procedures?" Brett asked.

"No. I'm good." Liam had already had enough of the niceties. "Lower level?"

Brett checked his tablet. "The Cascadian Salon." Then he added what was obviously a customary line. "Have a winning day."

"Thanks."

On the first floor was the boutique, where a wide array of luxury goods and collectibles were available for immediate purchase. Liam had bought more than one gift for his grandmother over the years from among the frequently rotating merchandise. On some of the upper floors were the personnel necessary to run this one location for the international operation that was this auction house.

In the back of the building and in the rear of the lower level were the auction rooms. They ranged from very large to extremely small, depending upon the type of items being auctioned and the size of the group of attendees invited or expected. Liam knew from experience that today's auction was likely to be small.

After being advised of the room number he needed, Liam made his way to the elevator tucked discreetly in the southwest corner. He could deal with tiny places again but preferred not to. He hadn't suffered the type of torturous PTSD that plagued so many other veterans, but memories of being trapped on that last mission still reared up when he least expected them. No point inviting them if he could avoid it.

Liam pushed through the door beyond the elevator and moved quietly down the steps. The staircase ended two flights down and he emerged into a tastefully appointed hallway. Elegant directional plaques affixed to the wall indicated the path to the room he sought.

He tucked his sunglasses in his pocket. The only noise in the hall was the quiet hum of the central air conditioning, so the loud metal squeal of the door hinges was startling when he pulled it open. Liam stepped through, letting the door close behind him with a dull thump.

A woman softly snickered. "No one can sneak in here, that's for sure."

He looked in her direction and it required effort to hide his reaction. Women who looked like her never showed up at events like this

– at least none he'd ever attended. If they did, he'd always attend in-person when he could, even if he had no interest in what was being auctioned.

Not that he was looking for a woman. Or a relationship. What he'd gone through after Kelsey had taught him that romance hurt like hell. It was something better experienced through words in a book rather than in person.

He wasn't going to risk going through that kind of pain again.

That didn't mean he didn't still appreciate beautiful women.

And this woman had plenty of reasons to be appreciated.

At first she seemed to be about 5' 7" tall, but then he realized her shoes were making up nearly four inches of that height. A snug, knee-length, gunpowder-grey skirt appreciated her curves in a way only well-tailored fabric could. Her hair was a glossy dark brown, and he noticed glimmers of auburn within it. The abundance of her tresses were gathered up at the back of her head in a way that was ordered enough to be professional, but relaxed enough to be casually sexy. If only she'd worn glasses, she'd have fulfilled a naughty librarian fantasy he hadn't even known he had until that moment.

"You'd think they could invest a few dollars on lubricant." As he said the words, he realized how they might sound to her, and quickly clarified, "WD-40. For the hinges."

Liam didn't know who was more surprised at his slightly awkward comment, him or her. A stodgy, high-end auction wasn't the place for innuendo, accidental or otherwise.

He held her honey-eyed stare, wondering if she'd reply to his words with outrage, offense, or if she would be obtuse about the double meeting in his words. She didn't miss a beat,

"Maybe I should do a good deed and loan them some. I usually have a tube in my purse," she said. Her lips quirked upward on one side, like she was resisting a laugh. "Lubricant, not WD-40."

Well, that was unexpected.

"Generous of you," he said at last.

"I try." She gestured with her chin in the direction over his shoulder. "You'd better check in, even if you're only here to watch."

The words were said with a slight but mischievous smile on plush lips that were tinted a rich red color. It reminded him of the wine his buddy liked to drink. Next time, instead of teasing Mason about his choice, he'd be thinking about her lips.

She turned around on her impossibly high heels and walked away. Rounded hips shifted hypnotically as she moved. When she'd been facing him, he'd struggled to keep his eyes respectfully above the generous curves that strained the buttons of her white blouse. During their all too brief encounter, Liam had noted manicured fingernails kept slightly long. The color matched her lips. There were no rings on her hands, which made him give a mental fist pump. They were soft-looking hands with long, slender fingers that would feel amazing wrapped around his --

"Sir, you have to register even if you're just observing." The comment was addressed to him, and the auction house representative sounded irritated. "We start shortly. You must register or leave."

"Got it," Liam said, pulling his gaze away from the beautiful stranger.

The older man shrugged and looked at her too, "I understand. I wasn't always this age."

"Never too old to appreciate beautiful women, huh?"

"Exactly. Just too old to appreciate them the same way I used to," the older man admitted.

Because Liam was pre-registered, it only took a few minutes to get his paperwork and bidding paddle in hand.

"I'm Tom, and I'll be here for the duration of the auction." The other man told Liam. "Any problems or questions, you can come see me or talk to another representative in the salon itself."

"Thanks, Tom." Liam leaned in a bit closer. "I have a permit to carry concealed, and I am. What's the current procedure here?"

"Speak to security at the metal detector and show them your paperwork."

Tom indicated a doorway across the room and a metal detector there, flanked by two security guards. It was a smooth process to get through security after Liam gave them his identification and quietly alerted them about his weapon. He was ushered smoothly around the detector, and into the larger room on the other side.

Liam had missed the auction item viewing opportunity that had been made available to bidders, but he'd looked over what was in preview online and read the comparative reports. The way modern auction houses simultaneously coordinated live streaming bids, regular online bids, and in-person bids was always impressive.

He already knew the item he wanted to win. It was a beautifully bound edition of romantic and other poetry written by Percy Bysshe Shelly and published not long after the poet's death in 1822. There was a chance the final price would end up outside his budget, but there was an equal chance he'd walk away with the book as his own.

The room was small compared to most venues for these things, but still large enough for at least four dozen chairs neatly set in rows. Each chair was a few feet from the one next to it, the placement clearly trying to make bidders feel they had a bit of privacy. Along one wall were auction house representatives standing with their clipboards and communication devices, ready to please bids by proxy for customers who couldn't be there in person.

The air was efficiently kept cool, providing a nice respite from the sweltering world outside the doors, and optimal conditions for the items up for bid. Each item would be brought out when it was officially presented and put up for auction. The atmosphere in the room buzzed with the excitement of the thrill of the hunt, money and stress, all tastefully subdued.

Liam was focused on acquiring a single, specific item. Nothing else.

Now, as he enjoyed the sight of the alluring woman again, he realized he suddenly had two interests today. Liam headed to the vacant chair closest to her. Her attention was now focused on the auction catalog, and it didn't escape his notice that she now wore eyeglasses with black frames.

Hello, naughty librarian.